MORE ABOUT
# THE AUTHOR

Tammy Hotsenpiller is a pastor, life coach, author, and speaker. As the founder and executive director of Women of Influence, a women's movement that educates, equips, and empowers women, Tammy has assisted numerous women in launching small businesses and following their dreams.

As a life coach she has coached CEOs of Fortune 500 companies and shared her wisdom on Fox and Friends, Fox News with Lauren Green, and contributed to Brooke Burke's *Modern Mom*. Tammy has also published six books: *Taste of Humanity, 3 Skips and a Jump to Becoming a Woman of Influence, Curious, The Park, Collinsville,* and *Lost in Manhattan.*

Tammy and her husband, Phil, live in Orange County, California, and adore their three amazing children, their equally incredible spouses, and six wonderful grandchildren.

# PRAISE FOR
# LOST IN MANHATTAN

Sometimes heartwarming and uplifting, sometimes raw with honest emotion, *Lost in Manhattan* is a beautiful story that inspires the reader to step forward in faith in the midst fear and uncertainty.

As a wife, adoptive mother, and attorney and after losing my mother when I was a teenager, I sensed an undeniable connection with Rachel D'Angelo. As she navigates through frightening circumstances we can all relate to, I felt peace knowing the fears and struggles I've been confronted with throughout my lifetime are common to so many others.

When life takes a turn we don't expect and leaves us lost and unsure of our future, how do we stay in faith? Rachel inspires the reader through her stunning resilience to push through fear, doubt and worry, leading to a life fully surrendered to God. *Lost in Manhattan* reveals how true love, joy and peace are found in God alone. Tammy provides inspiration for anyone feeling lost to lean into God, pursue a life of prayer, and trust the Holy Spirit to lead you back to life.

**Danielle Augustin**
Attorney, Speaker, Faith Writer/Blogger
Author of *Girlfriend Revival*

# LOST IN MANHATTAN

 TAMMY HOTSENPILLER

# LOST IN MANHATTAN

by Tammy Hotsenpiller

First Edition, January 2019
Copyright © by Tammy Hotsenpiller

 Published by Influence Media
8163 E. Kaiser Blvd., Anaheim, CA 92808

ISBN: 978-0-9987293-7-4

www.tammyhotsenpiller.com

# CONTENTS

"I will never leave you nor forsake you."

— Joshua 1:5

*As the Founder and President of* Women of Influence *it is my heart to champion and support women. This book is dedicated to all the women and men that have battled cancer. God is our healer and I have seen Him heal.*

A portion of the books sales will go to finding a cure for breast cancer.

— Tammy Hotsenpiller

# PREFACE

When I started on this journey three years ago to tell the story of Rachel D'Angelo I never anticipated it becoming a trilogy. I simply wanted to share my experience with Holy Spirit in the park. Sitting down at my desk, page by page, I began to pour out my heart. Rachel D'Angelo became my fictional character to share the intimacy I had experienced with Holy Spirit. The overwhelming response from women that had read *The Park* convinced me we were onto something. Women are looking for intimacy. Women are looking for authenticity. Women are looking for Holy Spirit.

I found it endearing that so many people asked me about the town of Collinsville located in upstate New York. It was such a quaint and special place. I knew I had to write a second book. *Collinsville* was birthed.

As we journeyed with Rachel D'Angelo through her infertility, adoption, and disappointment we became more attached to our character. It was as if Rachel was our best friend. The kind of girlfriend every woman wants—sophisticated, educated, kind, yet simple. Rachel's story was not over, because life is not perfect. We had to journey with Rachel through one more story. *Lost in Manhattan* was born.

I pray that through this book you will find Holy Spirit near and dear to your heart. At times we all feel lost. True to His word He will never leave us nor for sake us.

# ACKNOWLEDGEMENTS

Jessica Driskell, Executive Director of Women of Influence: Thank you for always being three steps ahead of me. You are more than a staff member you are a friend. Your 'can do attitude' and 'what's next' response has allowed me to accomplish so much more. You are a true blessing.

Marlene Tafoya, Lori DeAngelo, and Lisa Haines: To my three amigos, you ladies have been with me on this entire journey. Editing should be work but you made each chapter come alive. I am sorry the story is finished. But I am confident there will be another project on the horizon. I love you all so much.

Simone Genevieve Gabryk: You are brilliant. Thank you for the stunning book cover. The trilogy of book covers detail the story beautifully. You have a gift with design.

Arica Snyder and JD Davis, Jr.: Thank you guys for creating such a powerful promotional video. I have had so many people tell me they feel they are in the story when they watch the trailer. You are both such gifted people.

Angie Mathews: Thank you for your support and gift to edit. You have become my right arm as a writer. I know we have many more projects to tackle. Now let's go make a movie.

Holly Wagner and Teresa Adams: Thank you for sharing your story. Your bravery is what keeps us strong. Together we will find a cure for cancer and stand strong in our faith...that

God still heals.

Women of Influence: To my amazing friends, and leaders. Thank you for always supporting and encouraging me to go for more. This series has changed my life forever and you have been on the journey with me. I love you all.

My Tribe - Phil, Jeremy, Josh, Jen, Kim, Elisa, Brandon and my amazing grandchildren: Thank you for always loving me. I could not be more proud of each and every one of you. Reach for your dreams and then make new ones. Remember to enjoy your life and along the way work really hard. You have all my love.

Thank you Holy Spirit for birthing this story in my heart. My relationship with you has changed everything in my life.

*Holy Spirit inspired the story. I just told it.*

# FOREWORD

There were almost 300,000 diagnoses of breast cancer in 2018 and US Breast Cancer statistics say that one in eight women will develop the disease. In 2005, I became one of those women.

My journey included two surgeries, weeks in a hospital and dozens of doctors visits. I know that there are many of you who can relate to that journey, either because you have taken it, or have walked beside someone else.

I appreciate that Tammy is highlighting breast cancer in this book, and thought that I would share a few things I learned as I navigated cancer. I learned a few things along this road. Hopefully this helps you!

## Fear is real

Brave is more than a word. For me the best way to combat the fear was by putting my faith in what God says. Even this year as I went for my check up and faced the same hospital smells, I had to remind myself that fear is a liar — that Jesus paid the price for me to be whole — that I am strong and courageous.

## Together is better

I could not have navigated the battle successfully without the friends and family who were with me every step of the way. I didn't even know what to ask, but friends would show up with dinner or drive me to one of the many doctor's appointments. Although I have become better at asking, it was so nice when I didn't have to.

I learned to be OK with not getting the answer to "Why?" I think that was the beginning of my learning to trust God even when I didn't understand. I haven't arrived at perfection in this area, but I am better. And I think God is OK with that.

I gained a deeper revelation and even longing of Heaven. Heaven is the only place free from pain and suffering. Heaven is our home. Earth is our assignment. I prayed daily that I would be found faithful in my earthly assignment

**Laughing is essential!**
Find those people. Watch those movies.

**Find someone to help**
When we are in pain we can be selfish…well, maybe you aren't, but I was. Helping others was a huge part of my journey.

Just a few thoughts, love to each of you!

Xoxo

**Holly Wagner**
Pastor Oasis Church
Founder GodChicks/She Rises
Author *Find Your Brave*

At the young age of 37 years old, I heard the words, "I'm sorry, you have breast cancer!"

It's almost impossible to describe the flood of emotions that go through your mind and the conclusions you quickly empower. This was a far cry from the life I used to live as a pageant queen and one who lived a rather glamorous social life. I was just newly remarried and I wondered if my husband would still find me desirable? I questioned who would be able to raise my children? Regardless, I knew I was embarking on a very long and difficult road ahead of me.

I always had a strong faith in the Lord, but this is when I had to take it to a new level. I began to see how God was there through every struggle I felt. It was just a matter of letting him take over and carry me while I was too weak to walk on my own. Scripture continually reminded me of the promises that God had for me, to give me a future and a hope. I suddenly gained perspective on the definition of a true friend. My heart was so full from the outpouring of love that enveloped me. Not particularly from the ones you would expect either. Looking back regardless how difficult it was, I saw how Jesus orchestrated every step and I can truthfully say the journey was well worth it.

**Teresa Adams**
Wife, Mother, and Cancer Survivor

# CHAPTER ONE
## PASSING THE TORCH

"Rachel tilted her head back and inhaled the soft scent of lilac caressing her face. The sweet morning breeze surrounded her in an embrace, welcoming her to the park like an old friend.

Even with eyes shut tight against the rays of early summer sun, she felt the immense blessings before her. In the distance she could hear leaves dancing in the breeze, the gentle splash of people paddling around the lake, and the musical laughter of children. The sounds, beauty, and spirit that surrounded her warmed her heart and reminded her why she fell in love with Collinsville. But, most of all, she offered her deep gratitude for the two precious beings right before her.

Rachel held her breath as she listened to the serene murmurs coming from Skylark nestled in her stroller and the adorable coos of sweet baby Slater inside the wrap against her chest. She couldn't believe they were both sleeping so soundly at the same time.

"Dear Heavenly Father," she prayed silently. "I'm so grateful for...*everything*. There is too much to name. I'm so grateful for how well things are going at *Cali's* and for how expertly Maddy has stepped into her role overseeing things. Thank you for affording me this time to be at home with Sky and Slater. I'm so in love with being their mom and appreciate the opportunity to be with them."

She paused, considering her forthcoming request.

"You have blessed our family with so much, but, Lord, can you please help Cody? Work has been slow for him. I can tell he's eager to have new projects, new clients. Please be with him at his meeting today. Bless him with the opportunity to take on something new that he'll enjoy and that will provide our little family with a safety net. Thank you."

Finishing her prayer, she tried to lift her head, but found the gesture draining. She was exhausted. *No one will mind if I sleep like this for just a minute,* she told herself.

Just as she drifted into a light catnap, Skylark suddenly began to cry. Rachel's head snapped into place. Offering her a yogurt squeeze pack, she quietly tried to appease her while standing to bounce in an attempt keep Slater asleep. Wrapping an arm around him as she bobbed up and down, she felt something wet soaking through the wrap. Lifting the fabric, she peaked in to discover his diaper had leaked...everywhere.

"Blow out," she mouthed to Skylark, horrified.

Skylark stopped crying momentarily as though she conceived the magnitude of the mess before her. Her little eyebrow lifted, seemingly intrigued.

"Major blow out," Rachel said softly, appreciating the camaraderie with her 11-month-old daughter.

Skylark stared a moment longer and then her lower lip began to quiver.

"Oh, no, no, sweetie," Rachel pleaded. "Please don't cry. You don't want the yogurt? How about a banana? My phone? Do you want mommy's phone?"

Skylark launched into an even louder wail as Rachel scrambled to find something to distract her. Unable to calm her, Rachel tossed everything into the stroller's undercarriage and turned to race home, when suddenly Slater woke and joined the chorus. Feeling defeated and panicked, Rachel placed one hand firmly on the stroller and wrapped the other around Slater and sped home.

\*\*\*

Rachel woke to the distant sound of Cody animatedly reading "The Very Hungry Caterpillar." Momentarily confused, she recalled drifting off to sleep in the rocking chair after both kids went down for their afternoon naps. Cody must have carried her to bed. She caught a whiff of his special tomato sauce simmering and felt her stomach rumble.

Rachel smiled.

Then she frowned.

At once she felt grateful for Cody's extreme capability and embarrassed at her own failure. Why was it that her husband was able to manage both kids, happily, entertain them, make dinner, and put her to bed like a third child, while she could barely manage to get to and from the park without a complete emotional (the kids) and mental (her) breakdown?

\*\*\*

"You look like a new woman!" Cody exclaimed as she entered the kitchen.

"I feel like a new woman," she said.

Skylark was sitting in her highchair at the table, cheerfully picking at spaghetti noodles and pasta sauce while Slater sat happily in his swing. Walking over and giving them both a kiss, she slumped into a chair next to Skylark.

"I don't know if I can do this on my own," she said. "It's been so nice having you here more to help this past month. What'll I do when you get busy again in the fall and I'm all alone? By September, Sky's going to be a busy, walking 14-

month-old and Slater will already be four months old. He'll want way more interaction than hugs, milk, diaper changes, and tummy time, and Sky's going to be into everything. How will I manage?"

Cody's naturally upturned lips frowned with concern. "Rach, you're being too hard on yourself. You had a messy morning. Unexpected eruptions — tears, snot, throw-up, and *otherwise,* are just part of the territory. What I saw when I got home were two pristine, cherub-looking babes, dressed in fresh jammies, sleeping comfortably, safe in their beds, in a magazine-worthy nursery; and a mom who was wearing herself out making sure everything was perfect. You need to care for yourself too, you know?"

She nodded. "I know."

"I don't believe you," he said, brushing back a strand of her hair to look in her eyes.

She looked Cody deep in the eyes and took a breath. "I just feel so much obligation...," she started. "To them, to God. I prayed for a baby. *We* prayed for a child and were blessed with two beautiful children. They are both a gift from God. They are really His children and He has blessed me with the amazing gift of being their mom, and steward. I can't take any moment for granted."

Cody looked Rachel in the eyes. "You're His daughter too, Rach. God loves you. Just like He loves Skylark and Slater, He loves you. He wants your needs to be met, too. You need to make time for you. If you don't, you'll burn out," he said sternly.

She nodded again, knowingly. "I know you're right," she agreed. "It's hard to find time and I feel guilty making it a priority, but I'll try."

Just as Cody brought plates to the table, Slater let out a wail.

"Do you think he could be hungry?" she asked Cody.

"Maybe? Check his diaper."

Rachel picked up her tiny son. Bouncing him affectionately she placed his rear in front of Cody. "You check," she said with a smile. "I've had enough for today."

He laughed and took a look. "Clean as far as I can tell."

Rachel grabbed her nursing cover and returned to her seat at the table. Slater's cry continued to escalate as Rachel quickly got situated and struggled to get into position.

"You'd think I'd be an expert at this," she said, her voice croaky with stress. She turned to Skylark and stroked her soft brown hair. "It seems like mere months ago I went through this age with her, but nursing adds a whole other layer of complexity. It's really challenging."

"It *was* just mere months ago," he said. "I'm not saying that it's not hard to have two babies. I'm just saying you need to have a little grace with yourself."

Realizing she was famished, Rachel took a big bite of spaghetti and felt something wet hit her face. Turning, Skylark beamed with a smile, little hands full with a second round.

"We don't throw food, Sky. Are you all done?" Rachel asked. "If you're done, we'll get you in the bath."

Cody crammed a big bite of food in his mouth and stood to grab Skylark before she tossed more noodles. "Come here, princess. Time for a bath."

"You didn't get to eat anything," Rachel objected. "I can take her after I feed Slater."

Cody smiled. Holding Skylark on his hip, he grabbed a breadstick.

"Please eat," he said. "This was actually my second helping. I'll get her in the bath and then we can meet in the nursery in a few minutes to get these two munchkins to bed."

***

Feeling like cattle rustlers trying to sneak past the sheriff and her deputy, Rachel and Cody tiptoed out, gently closing the nursery door behind them. Waiting for a moment, they both exhaled when they didn't hear a peep.

Relieved and exhausted, Rachel playfully fell into Cody's chest. He wrapped his arms around her and kissed the top of her head.

"Should we try and watch some T.V. for a few minutes?" he asked.

"If there's ice cream, I'll watch any sport thing you want," she said with a smile.

"I was going to let you watch The Bachelor," Cody admitted. "But, maybe I'll get you a bowl of cookies and cream, then I won't feel bad if I flip back and forth at commercials."

As they made their way downstairs, Rachel felt herself reemerge. Realizing things other than baby meltdowns and catatonic naps happened that day, she quickly asked, "So, how'd your meeting go? I'm sorry I didn't ask sooner, just a little groggy."

Cody stopped mid-stair and hesitated momentarily.

"Was it not a good fit?" Rachel asked. "To be honest, I'm so grateful to have you home. I'll take you as long as I can have you."

Cody offered a half smile and continued down the stairs. Meeting at the bottom, he took her arm and guided her into the living room. Taking a seat together on the couch, he cleared his throat.

"I was going to wait until tomorrow to talk to you," he said. "After today, I didn't want to put any extra stress on you."

Rachel felt a pang of fear in her stomach. "What is it?" she asked.

"Well," he said. "The job's huge and appealing for a number of reasons, one of which are the opportunities it could open for future jobs. It's more than we've been praying for. It's truly an incredible blessing. But, it starts soon. And, I'll need to head to the city a few days a week. So, the hours will be long."

With each new reveal Rachel felt her stomach turn with dread. The prospect of being left alone without Cody's back-up was frightening.

"Oh, Cody," she said, doing her best to sound upbeat and share in his excitement. "That's wonderful. I'm so happy for you...for us. Do you know anything else? Can you give me any details?"

"It's a renovation project," he explained. "The operating company is taking a turn of the century building in the Arts and Craft style that's been neglected for more than 30 years and turning it into a hip hotel. They're looking to me to advise, consult, and manage all carpentry projects throughout."

"Wow," Rachel said.

Inside she was vacillating between extreme gratitude and disappointment. The job couldn't be more perfect for Cody. He was an encyclopedia of knowledge on all things from the Arts and Craft movement because he loved it. And, the managerial role was exactly what he had been looking for. While he did well with his commissioned pieces, the work was very labor intensive and not always consistent.

Sometimes he was booked out for months in advance and others, like recently, it was quiet. She and Cody had both been praying that he would receive a new opportunity, and this was a gift beyond measure. Rachel just wished he could consult from home, or at the very least Collinsville.

"God is good," she said, overwhelmed, but knowing she needed to have faith. "It's amazing the gifts He's blessed our family with."

Cody looked relieved and happy, which made Rachel want to be truly on board. She knew the job was a blessing. Plus, Cody deserved the chance to expand his career. Leaning forward he gave her a kiss.

"You're amazing," he said. "I know this can't be the best news for you to end today on, but I love that you can see the blessing that I think it is too."

"Remind me, how'd this company find you?"

"An old colleague from college contacted me," he explained. "She's the creative director for the project and when she was informed they were looking to maintain the authentic Arts and Craft character, she remembered me. As I'm sure you can imagine, I geeked out pretty hard on Arts and Craft in college when I discovered carpentry and woodworking. Everyone within earshot knew I was into it."

"Aw," Rachel cooed. "I *can* imagine. You're still a total nerd about it."

They both laughed, which made Rachel feel more relaxed, less conflicted about the opportunity.

"Did you have classes with her? Was she a good friend?" Rachel questioned.

"We had a few classes together, a few friends in common," he replied. "She was also working to get a BS in engineering. So, we had a lot of really stressful math classes together. Those classes are how I ended up in wood shop and she wound up in art and graphic design classes. Funny enough it appears our hobbies have become our careers."

"Well, you must have made quite an impression for her to remember you 10 years later," Rachel added.

"I guess," Cody replied. "I'm thinking it was just more out of need. There can't be too many of us in the Tri-state area."

"When will you start?"

"Two weeks."

Rachel sighed. "I'm ready for ice cream."

***

"Okay, milk's in the fridge for Slater. Skylark's breakfast and lunch are in there, too. Be sure to plate them like I showed you."

Cody gave her a crooked smile.

"If her food looks pretty, she's more likely to eat everything; not just the fruit," Rachel said, as she gathered her things.

Cody sat at the kitchen table casually sipping a cup of coffee with one hand, and rocking Slater in his swing with the other.

"We'll be fine," he said. "Get to *Cali's*. We'll walk over there to say hello in a bit."

"Thank you. Love you, guys. Tell Sky I love her when she gets up."

Rachel gave both boys a kiss and headed out the door.

It was a beautiful Tuesday morning. The sun was soft but bright, and birds were busy, welcoming the day with song. It felt good to get out of the house. It had been five weeks to the day since they had welcomed baby Slater home and Rachel missed the conversations with her team and customers. She

27

never realized how busy and involved she was in Collinsville community life, until she was on maternity leave and more or less housebound.

With Skylark, it had been an adjustment. The whole process leading up to adopting her had been incredibly stressful. But, it was that hardship and intensity that kept Rachel on the move and connected to good friends, like Susan Bishop. Plus, with Sky, Rachel had naiveté on her side. It always seemed like it would be just a few more weeks until she would feel like herself again. And, in a way it was.

After the adoption was official and everything they had been through with the agency was said and done, Rachel felt like an improved version of herself…like Rachel 2.0. Of course, she was now responsible for an amazing little human, which was intense, but the daily challenges and successes made her feel at the best times like a superhero and at the worst like she was learning and growing. Plus, her heart felt like it had doubled in size. With Slater, while her heart felt as though it had yet again doubled, she was physically different. Everything reminded her that things had changed.

Five weeks postpartum, Rachel was still healing. She had another week before she would be released by her doctor to take the *Holy Rollers* on a skate through the park. And, while breastfeeding provided an amazing, divine connection to Slater, it also tethered her to another human in a way she had never experienced. Rachel felt like she was learning to navigate these early months of motherhood all over again. But, even with all of the challenges, she had never felt more blessed.

It seemed as though God's gifts were limitless. Answers to prayers had been so abundant that after this last blessing, Rachel felt the need to step back and really consider what she was asking for. Waking up with the slightest hint of buyer's remorse for His most recent gift was a terrible feeling. But, she realized it wasn't about needing Cody at home. And, it wasn't about being disappointed with the new job. She was extremely grateful. It was just the thought of being on her own was...*lonely*.

What Rachel wanted was a tribe. She could never have dreamed motherhood would feel so isolated. She imagined a life where she actually had *a village* to help raise Sky and Slater, and it made her desperately miss her mom and Aunt Cali. Late at night, in sleepless delirium, she often had visions of the two sisters bickering over who got to take the next watch, begging Rachel to let them help with the bath, dinner, diaper changes, nap time, playtime, everything.

In her heart, she knew if things were different, that's exactly how it would be. She even swore she heard the jingle of Aunt Cali's bangle bracelets one night over the white noise of the baby monitor; but when she got to the nursery all she found were two peaceful, sleeping babes.

While she had a great group of friends in Collinsville, it wasn't the same as family. The management team at *Cali's Cafe and Boutique* were all very close, most notably Maddy whom Rachel considered a good friend; but they were also all young and focused on starting or finishing college, dating, and the like. The women from church, even Vera and Doris, had been there for Rachel through good and bad, but most of them were quite a bit older. Just like Cody's grandparents, who were his parents growing up.

They were wonderful. They leapt at the chance to help with their great grandchildren, but anything more than an hour or two and they were pooped. Her dad and Nancy were the closest thing, but they only made it up to Collinsville one or two days a month. And, Susan, her dear friend Susan Bishop, who had taken a sort of maternal, nurturing role in her life, lately seemed distracted, distant. Rachel hadn't seen in her a number of days and missed her frequent check-ins.

While Rachel knew any of them would help her out in a pinch, she yearned for a group of women to commiserate with, embrace, nurture, and love Sky and Slater as much as she did. She wouldn't shun any nurturing and motherly love for herself, either. Cody was more than she could have wished for. He happily helped everywhere he could, and while he really went above and beyond it felt like they were a team, in the trenches together. Lately, the kisses and hugs felt more like *good game* handshakes and high fives congratulating each other on another semi-successful day.

A soft breeze kicked up, whipping at Rachel's shirt hem and tossing her hair about her shoulders. Over the gust she heard a still, small voice emerge from within her heart, reminding her, "You have Me and I will help you through."

Chills ran down Rachel's arms and she felt *God bumps* breakout everywhere.

"Oh, Heavenly Father, thank you. Thank you for the reminder. I know you are here for me, it's just so easy to get caught up in the here and now, on what's difficult, and what's upsetting. It's so hard to slow down and listen for Your words of love and comfort. Thank you."

Rachel felt awash in love and support, which she needed more than she even realized. The feeling had become so foreign, she was taken back with the solitude and divine comfort that accompanied it.

Heading to work for the first time since Slater was born, she was filled with mixed emotions. Because, beyond just heading in for a shift to check-in, catch up, and visit with everyone, she was planning to officially hand over the reins to Maddy, her longtime assistant.

\*\*\*

After Skylark arrived, Rachel and Cody had been able to coordinate a three-day schedule in which she physically went in and worked, then she would do managerial things, such as creating schedules and handling payroll, from home during nap time and in the evenings. It had been ideal for her. The cafe had long hours, opening early and closing late, so Rachel was able to be flexible with both Cody and Sky's (ever-evolving) schedules. But, when the confluence of being pregnant, working, and missing Sky's first crawl, and later her first word ("Dada") merged, Rachel had to have a heart-to-heart with herself.

"I think I need to be a stay-at-home mom for right now," she remembered telling Cody.

"Are you sure?" he had questioned.

"I don't do anything halfway," she replied. "I've been able to sort of get away with it for the past six months because *Cali's* has been in the off season and I've only had Sky to care for. But, with two babies and *Cali's* heading into the busy, tourist season, I won't be able to do either well unless I'm completely dedicated to one."

Cody had smiled in agreement and given her very pregnant belly a gentle stroke.

"When will you ask Maddy to take over?" he asked.

Considering, she said, "Not until after my maternity leave. I want her to ease into it, experience it while I'm out, and then I'll talk to her once we're settled in with Slater."

\*\*\*

As Rachel approached the cafe, she couldn't believe the day had already arrived. It seemed like she had just been working with the team helping to put up the boutique's spring window display and developing Easter specials. Getting closer she noticed the cafe's chalk board advertising new drinks and *tonics*.

*What in the world are tonics?* Rachel wondered, a little taken back.

Stepping into the old, familiar space she was hit with the rich scent of coffee and steaming milk, the sounds of blending ice drinks, and friendly chatter of customers and baristas. But, she soon spotted a slue of new items in the cold case and an entirely new menu board with only a few of the classic coffee beverages she knew and loved.

"Medium raw cacao elixir with collagen is ready for Tina," shouted Nicky, one of the youngest baristas, from behind the espresso machine. When she spotted Rachel she started waving emphatically. "Rachel! Welcome back. Baby Slater is so cute!"

"Aw, thanks. It's great to be back," Rachel said with a smile and returned the wave as she darted into the back room.

"Rach!" Maddy exclaimed, getting up from the back desk. "So happy to have you back...so, what do you think? Is it too *woo-woo*?"

Rachel was grateful that Maddy understood that some of the changes could be a bit questionable. She was also a little unnerved that Maddy made all of the changes without running them by her first.

"I know you're probably wondering why I didn't run these ideas by you first," Maddy started, as though she could read Rachel's mind. "I wanted to take my management role seriously. You were on leave, and we needed to do something to boost sales; so I took a little inspiration from what's trending in the city, what's available from local farms, and folk medicine to reinvent our drink and food offerings."

Rachel was speechless. She felt so out of it. *Was this something that people were doing? Tonics, folk medicine, collagen, with coffee?* She was confused and conflicted. What would Cali do, she wondered.

"When did you make all these changes?" Rachel asked.

"About a month ago," Maddy said. "We presented it to customers as a limited-time offering at first. Just marketing it locally as a 'Wellness Weekend' and we rolled out a handful of drinks with adaptogens, a variety of organic milk options, and a bulletproof coffee. Then we worked with some local farmers to create amazing salads and wraps made using their local produce, eggs, meat, and stuff. We made sure to have options for vegetarians, vegans, paleo folks, and even ketogenic drinks and snacks."

"I'm sorry, *keto*-what?" Rachel asked feeling hoodwinked.

"It's a trending low carb, high fat diet," Maddy explained. "Anyhow, the weekend was so successful, we had people driving up from the city the following week because they had seen posts about it on social media. So, we've kept it."

Becoming annoyed with her matter-of-fact attitude, Rachel could feel her nerves getting shaky. She wondered if this was a sign that she needed to continue working. She felt shortsighted to think that she could pass the responsibility of maintaining *Cali's* to anyone other than herself. Her heart was beating incredibly fast, she felt like she had betrayed her dear Aunt for even thinking it was an option.

"Well?" Maddy inquired. "What do you think? Do you hate it?"

Rachel sat trying to calm her nerves and offer a clear, unemotional response. After taking a moment she said, "I'm not sure. I need to consider a variety of things, the most important one being what Cali would have thought. I'll take a look at the new menu, the books, see what sales have been like, talk to customers and sit on this for a few days. But, Maddy, while I value you taking the initiative, you also need to know when something should be brought to my attention or run by me first. This is one of those things that should have been run by me first. I don't even know what this stuff is that we're feeding to people. I mean, can we make people sick? Is it medicine?"

Maddy looked disappointed. "Sorry, Rach. I wasn't sure if it was going to work, so I didn't want to bother you. When it did, I thought you'd be as excited about it as me. I should have talked to you. Stefani can give you a rundown on all the herbs. They aren't dangerous, no more than coffee, anyway."

Rachel didn't know how to feel about bursting Maddy's bubble, but she couldn't dwell on it. She was too focused on the mantra repeating in her mind, *What would Cali do?*

Maddy paused, and then cleared her throat. "Have you stopped into the boutique, yet?"

"No. Why?"

"Well, we made a few changes there, too."

***

"They've added *butter* to coffee and herbs I don't even know how to pronounce," Rachel said, as she slumped into the nursery's rocking chair. "The salads and wraps are delicious, so that's good; but everything else...I'm just confused. It definitely doesn't feel like the cafe I left a month ago. It doesn't feel like *Cali's*."

Cody handed Slater to her and took a seat on the floor with Skylark.

"What about the boutique? Did they make changes there, too?" he asked.

"Yes!" Rachel exclaimed. "There are all these bath products and things for meditation, like floor cushions and incense. I don't know what got into them. It's almost as if they'd been planning it. The sales, for both the cafe and boutique, have definitely increased, but it feels like a coup."

"What would Cali think?" he asked.

Looking at Slater's sweet face, she smiled and shrugged. "I've been trying to figure that out all day."

"Cali was always a little *woo*," Rachel added with a sweet laugh. "But, she was first and foremost a child of God. While the boutique reflected her great style and inherent knowledge of what was on trend…the cafe was intended to be a gathering place. A place for the community to connect, enjoy, and commune together."

"Have any of the updates changed those things?" Cody asked.

"No, not really," Rachel sighed. "The girls were showing me all the trendy boutiques in the city that are selling similar items. They really have a good eye. I don't know. Part of me thinks Cali would love it, and part of me thinks she'd be as confused as I am."

"Didn't she used to go on yoga retreats to Mexico and stuff?" Cody asked.

"Yes," Rachel agreed. "She even went to a sweat lodge in New Mexico at one point. I don't know. I only have a few days to try and figure it out. I want it all taken care of before you start work."

Cody smiled and leaned forward to tickle Skylark, who burst into giggles. "The only thing you can do is pray about it. The changes they've made, while extensive, seem to be working…and when I think about Cali they don't feel too far off base. But, you need to make the decision. She left *Cali's* in your hands."

The words weighed on Rachel. He was right. Cali had entrusted her. Rachel felt the burden to care for what Cali had built. Looking at her beautiful family though, the trust actually felt like a burden for the first time.

***

Rachel used her entire walk to work as an opportunity to contemplate through prayer what she should do about the *Cali* dilemma. She was grateful for His support, as well as Cody's. Today had not been a planned day away from the kids. In her master scheme, she had handed the reins to Maddy yesterday and was free. But, as she appealed for His guidance and assistance, she understood even without the changes made to the cafe and boutique she should have anticipated a need for some transitional support.

She spotted the park. Looking at the time, she decided she had a few minutes to head to her favorite spot to pray.

Her brain felt as though there were squirrels on the loose chasing around her thoughts. She was having a terrible time focusing on the real question at hand. She kept thinking about the variety of ways her life could be impacted by the different outcomes. Rachel was annoyed that her plan was not going smoothly. She was conflicted about the changes her team had made and wasn't sure how to feel toward Maddy. And, she was feeling personally like a failure for not maintaining better control, or knowing without a doubt how to manage the situation.

The worst thing for Rachel was feeling like she didn't know her aunt. The woman she adored her entire life, the one who loved her unconditionally and put her life on hold to care for Rachel as her own, felt unfamiliar.

Getting situated on her favorite park bench, she peered about the lake and the lush meandering paths. Still early, there were very few visitors. She had passed a few joggers and could hear birds chirping, but there were no children out riding their bikes or people on the lake yet.

"Aunt Cali?" she called softly. "I miss you. If you can hear me, I miss you so much. I wish you were here. I wish you were here to meet Sky and Slater. I wish you were here to have coffee and dinners and summer barbecues with Cody and me. I feel like I've lost control in so many areas of my life and I don't know what to do. I wish you were here to offer advice, quote scripture, make cookies, but most pressing, I don't know how you'd feel about the changes the team has made. I believe they did it with a loving, well-intentioned heart…but, is it too crazy? Does it take away from what you intended? Is it still a place for community and conversation? Or is it trying to cater to trends and tourists? Am I letting you down by stepping away? Would you put Maddy in charge?"

Rachel took a deep breath.

"Lord, please be with me today as I try to make these decisions. Bless me with the ability to hear you and to know in my heart what Cali would have wanted. Thank you. In Your name, Amen."

Rachel stood and a gentle breeze tossed her hair, brushed at her face and then vanished. She felt reassured that He was listening and she was comforted by Holy Spirit's presence. Filled with faith that everything would work itself out, she made her way to work feeling lighter than she had when she entered the park.

As she approached *Cali's*, the air was filled with the soft music of beautiful Spanish guitar. There was an older gentleman set up in the cafe's courtyard strumming away as customers sat and enjoyed their breakfast food and beverages. Rachel had to admit it was lovely.

Stopping to listen for a moment, Joanna, a regular customer, approached her.

"Oh, Rachel," Joanna said, beaming. "The changes you and the team have made are just incredible. This cafe has always been a special place for Collinsville, but similar to cafes you would find in the city or something. Now, it feels like something truly special. The live music, new drinks, sweet gifts in the boutique…the *food*! It's all absolutely divine. A true gift to our little town."

Joanna took Rachel's hands in hers and shook them with gratitude and Rachel smiled unsure of what to say.

"I'm so glad to hear that," she stammered. "It's been the team's hard work."

Walking to the door, she was greeted by another regular, John. He was an old friend of Cali's. A fixture at every summer barbecue, John was also a fellow volunteer at the Collinsville Community Church and someone Cali really valued and trusted. Rachel braced herself, prepared to ask what he thought. He ushered her inside, holding the door.

As she opened her mouth, he beat her to it. "I'll tell you what, little lady," he said taking a sip of his coffee. "Your aunt would sure be proud of you. You've taken her vision and given it life."

With a nod of his head, he gave her a pat on the back and made his way out.

Rachel blinked.

"She'd be really proud of the way you're managing everything, too. You've pulled together a terrific team. They're at the top of their game even when you're not here. They really respect you...and the memory of your aunt, even the really young ones who never met her. Keep up the good work."

Feeling like she might topple over with shock and gratitude, Rachel held the door.

"Thank you," she replied. "That's just what I needed to hear."

# CHAPTER TWO
## BEHIND THE SMILE

Torn between going straight home to see Cody and the kids or making a pit stop at the park for prayer, Rachel paused to take a sip of her drink. It was one of *Cali's Cafe's* new concoctions, an *elixir*, Maddy promised would increase her milk supply. It tasted like hot chocolate with an earthy undertone. With a shrug, she took another swig and decided a quick stop into the park was best for everyone.

Cody had stopped in with the kids a few hours ago bearing home baked cookies and handpicked flowers. They had just spent time in the park feeding the ducks and looked fresh as daisies. After the cafe, they planned to pick up something special for dinner. *Super dad*, Rachel thought with a laugh. Maybe he should stay home and she should go back to work full-time. But, the idea left as quickly as it entered her mind. The confirmation was clear: *Cali's* was in good hands, and while she felt in over her head, Rachel was in good hands, too.

"Oh, God," she sighed, taking a seat on her favorite bench. "Thank you so much for your mercy and graciousness. I'm overwhelmed by your love and the blessings you've shown me and my family. Thank you for helping me to know with a surety that I am making the right decision for *Cali's*. I am so excited to tackle motherhood with your support and guidance. I understand that as a mother to Sky and Slater, I'm playing a central role in your plan and I am so grateful for the confidence. Thank you for Cody. He's so capable and willing…I know I can learn from him and lean on him when needed. I'm truly blessed to have him as a husband. Please be with us as we prepare for his new job and the changes it will bring. I love you, Lord. In Your name, Amen."

***

When Rachel reached the house, the summer sun was dipping. Opening the front door she anticipated lots of noise, Cody cooking, Sky babbling, Slater yelling for milk, music playing, but it was eerily quiet.

"Hello?" she called softly.

Stepping into the kitchen she could see a prepared salad and strawberries on the counter. Grabbing a berry, she wondered where everyone could be when she heard Cody's voice out on the back deck.

"Yep," he said. "I've spoken with my wife and I'd like to accept the offer."

Rachel peeked through the window and could see him out back standing over the barbecue with tongs in one hand and his cell phone in the other. Skylark was in her playpen, happily eating a strawberry of her own, and Slater was in his swing, napping.

"Um," she heard Cody reply, seeming unsure. "We haven't quite finalized the child care situation. It'll be tough to get to the city again this week."

His awkward response piqued her interest, she wondered what the new job was asking.

"Let me talk to Rachel," he added. "I'll let you know Thursday if I'm able to make it."

Seeing him set down his phone, she made her way out the back door. Wrapping her arms around his waist, she gave him a big squeeze and felt him tense in surprise.

"Well, hello!" he said. "Dinner's almost ready."

"Everything okay?" she asked.

"Yeah," he said unconvincingly. "I just called Simone to let her know I was accepting the job offer. She asked me to come to a team dinner Friday night."

As Rachel walked over to pick up Skylark, she felt herself unwillingly bristle at the news. She couldn't tell if it was the name 'Simone' or the request for dinner Friday night that bothered her more; but neither made her feel good. She gave Sky a kiss and held her a little tighter.

"Do you feel like you should go?" Rachel asked, trying her best to sound neutral.

"No," he said bluntly.

"Really?" she asked relieved, but also concerned he wasn't putting his best foot forward.

"Yeah," he said. "It's just a networking thing. Nobody's done any work on the project yet. I don't need to build relationships with these people until I, and they, have something to show for it. It's definitely not worth a trip to the city…or a night away from my family."

He plated the perfectly grilled salmon and made his way into the house. Rachel suspected there was something more. He was irritated or bothered by something, but she would give him space. He could talk to her about it when he was ready.

***

Cody was already awake when Slater's cries for his 3 a.m. feeding woke Rachel. She was surprised to find him propped up on a pillow looking at his phone.

"Is everything okay?" she asked, as she got out of bed.

"Just having a hard time sleeping. Did you want me to get Slater? Bring him to you so you could feed him in bed?"

"It'll just be a few minutes," Rachel said. "I'll bring you some chamomile tea on my way back."

When Rachel got back to the room, Cody was asleep.

She set the tea on his bedside table and noticed his Bible laying open. He had underlined a verse, Proverbs 10:9, *"Someone who walks with integrity will be safe, but one who follows a crooked path will fall into the Pit."*

He had made a note in the margin *"No matter the circumstance, if we walk with integrity, we will be safe."*

Rachel was perplexed. She hated to think he felt fearful and wasn't talking to her, but she also knew she could be reading into something all wrong. She placed in a page marker and shut the Bible. It was nearly 4 a.m. Glad he was finally sleeping, she wondered if he was just worried about the new job or if there was something about the new job worrying him. Exhausted herself, she nestled into her pillow and quickly drifted off.

***

Rachel felt inspired for the first time in months. Having received spiritual confirmation that she was doing the right thing with *Cali's*, she was finally ready to dive into motherhood full time. And, once she had established to forge ahead in the new direction, she was pleasantly surprised to find she actually felt more like herself again.

There was something about having made a decision that allowed her heart and soul to be at peace — and the peace provided her space, allowing herself to reemerge. Cody seemed to be trying to soak up every minute with the family before starting the new job and Rachel reveled every moment as well, even if she did feel some underlying concern.

There hadn't been any discussion about what was bothering him, but Rachel figured it was just a fluke since he hadn't had any more rough nights. She would be a liar though if she said the Bible verse hadn't remained in the back of her mind.

Given the green light by her doctor to start exercising, Rachel took advantage of Cody's availability to watch the kids and got back into her fitness routine. Taking the Holy Rollers for a skate through the park or going for a power prayer walk were her top choices, although both seemed to highlight Susan's recent absence. Rachel loved to involve her dear friend in her special activities and lately it seemed she could only get her voicemail.

With Susan missing and Cody on his way to starting the new job, Rachel was lining up a full schedule to avoid falling back into a place of isolation. She had her dad and his wife Pam coming out for a couple of days, play dates planned with other young moms from church, a weekly baby music class in Poughkeepsie, and lots of developmental activities and park time planned for the kids and herself.

***

Getting up at 4 a.m. was nobody's idea of fun, but Cody needed to be into the city by 8 a.m. and didn't want to risk being late. Rachel was up nursing Slater when he was ready to head out. Cody came into the bedroom to say good-bye and Rachel felt awful when she saw his puffy, bloodshot eyes.

"Did you sleep?" she asked.

"Sort of," he said with a weak smile.

"Is it going to be like this every day?" she whispered.

"No. I just need to get the lay of the land, meet the team, start off on the right foot. You know? I'm going to miss you guys. I will probably be home around 8 p.m. tonight. So, I don't think I'll see Sky at all today. Give her kisses for me, and raspberries...give her a big, wet raspberry right on her bee-bo."

"Her what?" Rachel asked, stifling a laugh.

"Her belly button," he said, looking heartbroken. "Once I get situated, I can't imagine having to go in more than two days a week. On the days I do, I'll take the train. That way I can FaceTime with you guys, read, work, or rest to be refreshed when I get home."

"Sounds like a plan," she said leaning forward and giving him a kiss good-bye. "Love you. Text when you get there."

Watching him pull down their long, gravel drive she sighed. She could tell he was nervous, which was understandable, but deep down she questioned what he was nervous about exactly. Was it the job, the drive, the situation, or the decision?

She placed Slater back in his crib and wondered if they were doing the right thing. It all seemed to come together so easily which they both had automatically attributed to God and prayer, but were they being deceived? Was he putting himself in a bad situation? Rachel wasn't sure why, but she had a feeling there was something about the job that had Cody on edge.

***

"How was it?" Rachel asked softly as Cody hobbled into the house at 9:15 p.m.

"It was good," he said opening the fridge and staring a bit delirious. "I'm sore though. On my feet for close to nine hours and then crunched into a car seat for a 6-hour round trip commute...it's a long day. I knew it would be, but in practice it's even more than I anticipated."

"Are you hungry? I have a plate of food for you," she said. "It's in the Tupperware container in the fridge. Just pop it in the microwave for four minutes."

"I had a little something on the drive home," he said. "I think I just want a bowl of cereal. I feel like I need sugar."

Rachel raised an eyebrow. "That bad, huh?" she asked, knowing Cody only did treats on special occasions or when he was really stressed.

She met him in the kitchen and grabbed a bowl. "Do you want chocolate puffs or marshmallow stuff?"

"The marshmallow one…we have cereal like that in the house?" he asked surprised.

Rachel smiled. "Uh-huh. They were left over from the Easter treats I made for church…but I might grab a handful now and then."

"Come sit on the couch," she added, handing him a big bowl. "I'll give you a massage."

Cody sank into the cushions and reluctantly let Rachel work out his neck and shoulder muscles.

"What does tomorrow look like?" she asked.

"The same," he said robotically.

Rachel couldn't even comprehend it. When was he going to see the kids, she wondered.

"I just need to get through this week and I'll get everything figured out," he added.

"You have to go to the city *every day* this week?" Rachel asked stunned.

"Not every day…I don't think," he said, wavering. "There is just a lot of initial work that needs to be done on site. Today, I spent the entire day assessing the condition of the first floor. I have to look at everything from the staircase to the library bookshelves, the doors and floors…there's a lot of wood."

Rachel's heart sank. She hadn't really considered the work he'd be doing onsite. She figured he would go and do a quick once over and then be spending most of his time compiling a report of recommendations.

"The grandeur and quantity of it all diminishes the higher you go," he added. "The upper floors, don't have nearly as much; but it's going to take a lot of work to determine the condition of everything. Once I get the evaluation completed, I'll be preparing a report and recommendations – which can all be done from home."

Cody groaned.

"It's a lot, Rach," he continued. I'm going to be commuting almost daily for the first few weeks. We'll find a rhythm. It just takes time. It's an inspiring building though. I'm so honored to have the opportunity to bring its beauty back to life."

Rachel gave his shoulders a squeeze and rested her head on his arm. She was at a loss for what to say. The dream job was quickly turning into a nightmare as far as she was concerned.

"We need to figure out when you'll see the kids," she said, trying hard to not say anything negative. "Maybe we commute to the city one-day-a-week or something to do lunch with you."

"Let's get through this first week and talk about it this weekend," he said. "Day one was enlightening. I'm sure by Friday I'll have an even better grasp on what the day-to-day will look like."

"Okay," she said softly. "You ready for bed?"

***

Rachel could feel Cody toss and turn the entire night. Every movement sent waves of stress through her body. Concerned with how tired he already was and knowing he had another full day ahead, she was up all night right alongside trying to think of anything that would help. Nothing came to mind and fearful that talking to him might make it worse, she pleaded with God to offer Cody some mercy and some quality sleep.

When his alarm sounded at 4 a.m., Rachel was part relieved and part disappointed that his suffering in bed was over. She was pretty sure he had just really fallen asleep an hour or two before.

"How are you?" she asked in a whisper.

He rubbed his face and sat up.

"I could use a few more hours of sleep," he said. "I was going to wait until next week, but maybe I should try the train today."

"I'll look at the schedule," Rachel said. "Go get ready."

When Cody came out he looked tired, but pulled together. Rachel could hear Slater starting to wake over the monitor.

"There's a train leaving about every 20 minutes and it takes under 2 hours to get to Grand Central. You should do it. You can leave as late as 6:15 a.m. and still make it into the city before 8 a.m. You can sleep on the train, read, relax… stretch your legs."

He nodded, obviously exhausted. "Yeah, I've got to do something different. I feel like I'm going to be worthless and it's only my second day."

She gave him a kiss and raced to get Slater who was starting to cry. Meeting Cody in the hall on his way out, she tried to get Slater to turn toward his dad; but he was only interested in eating.

"I love you," she said. "Good luck with the train. I think it's the perfect alternative…it will alleviate a lot of the issues you had yesterday."

Cody gave her a kiss and stroked Slater's head. "I'll plan to FaceTime with you guys on my way home."

As the door closed and Rachel watched him drive away again in the deep dark early morning, she shuddered. It was a cold chill that made her feel like something was not right.

"Father, please be with Cody today. Keep him safe. Keep him strong. Keep him in your hands."

Taking Slater back upstairs, she was grateful she had a few hours to sleep before he and Sky were up for the morning.

***

With Slater happy in his swing and Skylark busy munching a breakfast of strawberries, Cheerios, and yogurt, Rachel nervously eyed the clock: 7:49 a.m. *He should have texted by now,* she thought. Rather than wait and wonder, she picked up her phone and called.

"Hi Rach," he answered, sounding stressed.

"Hey, just wanted to check in. Where are you?"

She could hear him exhale with exasperation. "I had to drive," he said. "I've been looking for a parking spot. Just found one. I'm here. I'll call at lunch. Love you."

Rachel looked at her phone, surprised he had hung-up. Totally bewildered, concerned, and feeling a little jilted, she didn't understand why he had to drive. She turned on the morning news and the lead story answered her question.

"An MTA worker died this morning after a fall, suspending service and leaving a number of commuters stuck for hours," read the morning news anchor with a solemn face.

Rachel immediately shut the T.V. off.

"You guys," she said to Sky and Slater. "Daddy's too tired to have driven! This week is *not* off to a good start."

She took a seat and rapped her nails on the table trying to think of a way to help. Looking over at Skylark, Rachel giggled when she realized she was trying to copy Rachel's hand with her little fingers.

"Thank you, sweet girl, I needed a little laugh," Rachel said. "So, what do you think? How can we help daddy?"

"Dada," Sky repeated.

"I bet you miss him, huh? You haven't seen him in two days. We could go to the city…get a hotel for a couple of nights? Then we could see dad, he could get some sleep, and it could give us a couple days to figure things out?"

Rachel shrugged as Skylark started to play with her remaining yogurt, splattering the kitchen like an expressionist artist.

"But, Grandpa Joe and Pam are on their way here, and we'd miss our first music class…and it's not sustainable. It's not a solution," Rachel said feeling discouraged.

"Ooh, but wait," she added excitedly, snapping her fingers. "It's not a perfect idea, but it's a decent idea…"

Skylark stopped playing with her yogurt and watched as Rachel picked up her phone.

"Hello? Dad?" she said into the receiver.

"Hey, Princess. We're well on our way. We should be there in about 30 minutes," Joe said cheerily.

"That's great. We're so excited to see you. I had a quick question. Cody's had a rough start to the week and has not gotten much sleep. I know he was hurting today. Do you think it would be possible for him to stay at your place tonight?"

"Aw, I'd love to, Princess. I'm just not sure how we'd get him a key. We don't have a spare with anyone in the city."

Rachel made a sad face at Skylark in disappointment. "Thanks, dad. Thought I'd give it a shot. I'm going to try to talk him into getting a hotel tonight. Poor guy just needs to get some sleep."

***

When Cody got home at 9:30, the kids were asleep and Joe and Pam were nodding off on the couch.

"Hey," Rachel whispered. "What can I get you? I've got a glass of warm milk with honey ready – it's supposed to help you sleep. Are you hungry? How was today?"

Cody looked at her, his eyes tired, and he smiled. "Thanks, Rach. I'm okay. Tired, but fine. If I get a good night sleep tonight, I should be able to make it through the week."

Joe woke up and gave Cody a wave.

"Hey, champ. Work looks good on you. Hardens up some of those pretty boy features," he said with a laugh. "Go get some sleep."

Cody smiled and nodded. "Will do, Joe. Thanks for coming out. It's nice to know you and Pam are here while I'm away."

Rachel handed him the milk and walked him upstairs. Giving him a kiss, she helped him out of his shoes.

"Same schedule tomorrow?" she asked.

"Yeah."

"Should you take some extra clothes? Just to have with you? In case you decide a hotel's a good idea?" she asked.

"No," he replied. "I'm going to try the train again tomorrow. Had it worked today, I think it would have made things a lot better."

"Okay. How is it? Do you like the people you're working with? Is it fun to be with someone from college?"

Cody cleared his throat seemingly trying to figure out how to answer the questions.

"Um, it's good," he said. "Everyone's really nice from what I can tell. I haven't spent much time with anyone aside from Simone, who I'm working closely with. It's not what I expected, but so far, so good."

Rachel felt her heart sink. It was a visceral reaction that surprised her. She wasn't sure what bothered her, Cody's hesitation or the name *Simone*.

"Is Simone the college friend?"

"Yeah," he said, followed by a big yawn.

Rachel felt conflicted. If she was honest, she was already starting to hate this job. On one hand, it was good because it occupied her mind not leaving any room for fear of the transition, on the other hand it was terrible because over the past two days all she could think about was hating the job and wanting Cody back in Collinsville. It's short-term, she told herself. It won't last forever.

"Get ready for bed," she said. "I'm going to make sure my dad and Pam have everything they need and I'll be up to come to bed, too."

"Sounds good," he said, taking a sip of the warm milk.

***

When Rachel got back upstairs, Cody had passed out. She did her best to move him into a comfortable position and got herself ready for bed. Crawling under the covers and turning out the bedside light, she closed her eyes and prayed silently for a better day tomorrow. She prayed that God would bless them both with peace for the way things currently were, but with the discernment and understanding to make changes as needed. Closing her prayer, she took solace in Cody's deep, steady breath and feeling his strong, still body beside her. She quickly drifted off to sleep.

She woke at 1 a.m. to Slater's cries and was happy to find Cody still sleeping soundly. When she woke again at 4:30 for another feeding, she was surprised to find Cody still asleep.

"Cody?" she said. "Hey, should you be up?"

He shot up and looked at his phone.

"I didn't set my alarm," he said instantly on edge. "I have to hurry."

"Remember you're taking the train today, so you should have extra time," Rachel said.

"Yeah, that went well yesterday," he said. "I need extra time for unexpected stuff like that. I wanted to be early today. Some of the key investors for the project are going to be onsite today and wanted to be prepared to share some of my initial suggestions."

Rachel was disappointed that she was only now hearing about Cody's big day ahead.

"Let me hurry and feed Slater and I'll get you a coffee and some egg and toast to-go, so you don't have to stop anywhere," she said.

Cody grabbed her hand as she headed to the hall.

"Rach, I love you. I'm sorry this is so stressful this week. I'm sorry I'm so stressed."

He looked like he wanted to say more, but Slater's cries were escalating.

"I love you, too. We'll figure it out," Rachel said on her way out. "We always do."

***

It was a gorgeous summer evening in the backyard. It reminded Rachel of when she would spend summers at Aunt Cali's as a little girl. Fireflies were darting about, the barbecue

53

was hot, and the multitude of conversations around her were friendly and Christ-focused.

Rachel kept wavering between extreme happiness in the moment, sentimental nostalgia, and sadness because Cody wasn't there to participate. But, watching Skylark's face as she became aware of the bugs' flickering lights, continued to bring Rachel back around to happiness.

After Cody's first week on the job, they had a big heart-to-heart Saturday morning after the kids went down for their naps. The commute wasn't working. Cody wasn't benefiting by returning home every night. He was too tired to hold a conversation with Rachel and wasn't getting to see the kids. It was presenting an unnecessary strain during a time that was already incredibly stressful.

They both agreed that something else needed to happen. They discussed options for heading to the city as a family, asking her dad and Pam if they could stay a few nights a week at their place or renting a place of their own for three months. They then broached the idea of having Cody stay by himself at Joe and Pam's place on his own or getting a hotel room a couple of nights a week.

Nothing felt like a great fit. The idea of commuting with two babies, and all their *stuff*, a few days every week was daunting. Her dad's place was tiny and while she knew they'd be welcome, it seemed like too much of an imposition. A lot of the other ideas sounded expensive and while it was possible, it seemed to defeat the purpose of the job in the first place. When Rachel felt as if all ideas had been exhausted, Cody hesitantly mentioned one of the project's key property investors had been friendly and made him an offer in passing.

"What'd he say?" Rachel asked.

"Well, it was just as we were finishing up lunch on Thursday," Cody explained. "I'm not sure how serious he was. He mentioned that he'd done my commute a few times and was surprised I was still standing. He offered me a room for the duration of the project at one of his other properties in the city."

"Offered you a room?" Rachel asked, shocked. "For free? Why didn't you say anything?"

Cody shrugged and offered her a disappointed half smile. "I was sort of hoping that it wasn't an option we were considering," he said. "I feel like a huge jerk for underestimating the commitment this job requires."

Rachel gave him a big hug.

"We're all doing the best we can," she said. "I can feel it. Can you? Holy Spirit is with us. He'll comfort and guide us through this tough time if we work to keep Him with us. I hate the idea of having you away for a few nights a week, but after this week...I prefer it to watching you stumble in and out of the house in the dark. It's only three full days a week that I won't see you. I think we can do this."

Cody had reluctantly agreed. It made the most sense for him to head to the city late Sunday afternoon and to return Thursday evening after work. He would work from home on Fridays drafting the report and have the rest of the weekend to spend with the family.

"It still sounds brutal," Rachel said.

"Yeah," he agreed. "Yeah, it does."

So, Rachel sat at the first Sunday potluck of the summer as a single mom, feeding Slater under a nursing apron and watching Skylark play happily in her penned-in area. While they typically started Memorial Day weekend on Saturday, this year's start was a little late because of everything going on in Rachel and Cody's life. But, it felt so good to have everyone over. The spirit the Collinsville community brought to her home was energizing and Rachel knew Cali would be so happy that she was carrying on the summer tradition.

Amidst all the camaraderie and fellowship, Rachel kept a look out for Susan Bishop. Her friend was not one to miss a party, and parties were never quite the same without her vibrant energy. Rachel had inquired with a few of the church members as to whether she was coming, if they'd seen her, if they knew how she was doing; but the story was more or less universal — no one had heard from her.

So, when Susan and Pastor Bishop walked into the backyard just as the party was winding down, Rachel was ecstatic.

"Hello!" she cried, standing to go greet them. "I'm so happy to see you."

Susan offered her giant grin and brought Rachel in for a big hug. "Oh, let me see this charming boy. I've missed him so. And, Sky? Where's she? I just want to drink them both up," she said delightfully. "And, you, my dear…how are you? I'm sorry I've been out of touch for the past couple of weeks. We were hit with some news and things have just been a little chaotic."

Susan's tone was as upbeat as ever, but there was something off. Rachel could sense it.

"Well, I'm so glad you two were able to come tonight. Come over and see Skylark and I'll get you some food."

"Oh, don't trouble yourself," Susan replied picking up Sky, instantly making the little girl giggle and smile. "Food is just not agreeing with me lately. Nothing wants to stay down…that is except vanilla milk shakes, which feels really odd for me, the health nut, to say."

Taking a closer look at her extremely fit friend, Rachel could see that she was thinner and her eyes were ever so slightly sunken.

"What's going on, Susan?" she asked with concern. "Is everything okay?"

Susan smiled brightly. "Everything's fine, sweetie. I'm so happy to see you and be here with these kiddos. Where's Cody?"

Rachel grimaced. "Oh, it's a long story and I need to get these two upstairs for bed soon. Are you free to meet up tomorrow? We could attempt a prayer walk together at the park? Or just meet up for coffee at *Cali's*?"

"I would *love* that," Susan said. "Let's meet at the park, whatever time's best for you."

# CHAPTER THREE
# TRUTH & TEARS

"So, how's it going?" Rachel asked looking at the digital image of Cody on her phone.

It was difficult to see if he was distracted or twitchy because it wasn't a great Wi-Fi signal.

"It's okay," he said. "The room is really nice. I've got a great view of the Hudson. But, it's weird being on the 36th floor. Quiet. Really quiet. No crickets, cicadas, nothing."

Rachel smiled.

"Yep, it's a different world," she agreed. "You should hear it when it's snowing. Even more silent. It feels like you're in a cocoon when you're that high up."

She paused. "The kids miss you. Sky's been saying 'dada' on repeat."

Cody looked sad.

"Yeah, I was hoping to catch them. I miss them, too. I'm sorry I'm not there to help finalize plans for Sky's birthday party. Are we still just planning to do a family thing Thursday and then celebrate with everyone else on Saturday?"

"Are you going to be home in time on Thursday?" Rachel asked. "I was just planning to do a little special dessert or something on Thursday and not celebrate anything until Saturday."

"That sounds good," he said. "It would be tough to get home in time. I know she won't know, but it still feels pretty terrible to blow off her first birthday."

"We can make it up to her when it counts," Rachel said, tiring of the topic.

She agreed. It *was* disappointing. It made her sad, too. She planned to make it a special day, but felt like she needed to walk the fine line of protecting Cody's feelings. He didn't want to know he was missing out on anything, but life couldn't be on hold because they had decided to live apart for a duration.

"How're you doing?" Cody asked.

"Fine," she said. "The Sunday potluck was fun. Everyone showed up, even Susan and Pastor Bishop. I'm actually going to go on a prayer walk with her a little later this morning. We'll see how that goes with the kids. I think there's something going on with her."

"Like something bad?" Cody asked, concerned.

"Yeah, I got the impression she had gotten some bad health news, maybe. I've grown pretty good at reading this stuff."

"Ah, Rach, I'm sorry. I know you really love Susan," he said, looking at his watch.

"Uh-huh," she agreed. "I'll see what she has to say. You need to head out. It's getting late."

"I love you," he said. "Please give the kids kisses for me? What time should I try tonight?"

"It seems 6 p.m. is always safe. It'll be bath time."

"Oh man, I'll try," Cody said disappointed. "But, I don't know if I'll make it. Gary, the guy who's set me up with the hotel room, wants to do dinner. He has some ideas he'd like to run by me."

"Really?" Rachel asked, surprised. "Well, that's great. Right?"

"Yeah, I think so. I don't know. I want to see my kids. But, yeah, work-wise I think it means he likes what I'm doing and trusts my opinion."

"Okay, well, good job," she said, giving him a cheesy thumbs-up. "Just text me when you get back to the hotel and I'll let you know if they're awake. Love you."

She blew him a kiss and he pretended to catch it.

"Dork," she said as the screen went black. Not a second later, she could hear Skylark over the monitor.

"Mama, ma ma ma," she babbled happily to herself.

Rachel's heart dipped, she would have to be diligent about getting the kids on a more regulated schedule. It was best for them, her, and Cody. Otherwise she envisioned the next three months being a bunch of near misses, frustration, and tears, from all parties involved.

*** 

The summer humidity had arrived in Collinsville with a vengeance. Rachel kept looking in the stroller to make sure Slater and Skylark weren't melting. She was eager to spend time with Susan, but wished they would have planned the walk for a cooler part of the day.

As Rachel made her way across the street toward the park, she could feel her heart speed up. Concerned with what Susan was going to tell her, the thought of a health issue and potentially losing another woman she loved dearly was almost too much to bear. She felt like she had suffered enough with losing her mom and then her dear Aunt Cali. And, if she was being honest with herself, it made her feel cursed. It was as if any woman she admired, loved, looked up to, and found solace with was doomed.

Taking a deep breath, she stepped through the park's entry gate and made her way down the charming path to their meeting spot by the lake. She felt a wisp of cool air blow past, softening the intense morning humidity and offering both physical and emotional momentary relief. She could hear, carried on the breeze a reminder to *Fear not. I am with you. I am with Susan. I am with Cody.*

Rachel took a deep breath and was filled with gratitude and calm. She could see Susan already sitting on a bench by the lake.

"Hey!" Rachel said trying to be enthusiastic and quiet. Both Slater and Skylark had just drifted off for their mid-morning nap and she was hoping to keep them asleep for at least a little bit.

"Hello, sweetie!" Susan replied in a hushed tone. "Aw, they are just *angels*! Look at them. Do you just love it? I know it's hard...but amazing, right?"

Rachel nodded. "It's definitely the toughest job I've ever had, but also the most rewarding. I do love it."

Susan took her hands and pulled her in for a big hug. "I've missed you, girl. So, Cody's out of town? For work?"

Rachel swallowed feeling some unexpected emotion bubble to the surface.

"Yes," she said. "It wasn't what we planned, but he recently accepted a 6-month consulting job in the city. We were under the impression that most of it he'd be able to do from Collinsville — which is true — it's just he won't be doing the main reporting portion until a little later into the job. For right now, he has to be on site to evaluate everything and get the information he needs to start the report. So, after a terrible week of commuting and a serious heart-to-heart we decided it was best if he stay in the city Sunday nights through Thursday afternoons for the foreseeable future."

"Oh, honey," Susan said looking saddened by the news. "I'm sure that was a very hard decision. How has it been?"

"It hasn't been that long, but it's stressful and hard. I'm glad that he's not doing the commute anymore. It was awful. But, I keep wondering if the job is worth this sacrifice."

"Sounds like a prayer walk will do us both some good," Susan said starting to walk. "I know I need some divine direction."

Rachel turned to try and catch Susan's eyes, but she was being uncharacteristically evasive.

"You always do this to me," Rachel said sweetly. "You make me feel like I'm the most important one in the room and the conversation always focuses on my stuff. I've been on edge since last night to hear what's been happening in your life these past few weeks."

"Well, sweetie, I haven't wanted to worry anyone, so I've just been laying low," Susan said softly. She pulled out a tissue and balled it in her hands. "About a month ago I went in for my annual mammogram and the results showed some abnormalities. After a biopsy and further testing I'm coming to grips with the fact that I have stage-four breast cancer."

Rachel's heart jumped to her throat. She felt ill. She had no familiarity with cancer and the word alone sent chills down her spine. She knew enough to know that stage four was not good. She said a fleeting, silent prayer and took a breath.

"Susan," she said, softly. "I'm so sorry."

Susan offered a conflicted smile and dabbed at the corner of her eye.

Immediately going into her default mindset when dealing with challenging situations, lawyer-mode, Rachel asked, "What are the next steps? What needs to happen to beat this?"

Susan beamed. "That's what I was hoping for. I love your grit. I'm going to need it, girl. So far the doctor's are giving me very grim odds. With the traditional methods, they don't think we'll be able to make progress fast enough…it's very aggressive. I need to get into a clinical trial if I'm going to beat this."

"Are you saying I can help by doing research and presenting a case?" Rachel asked excited.

"Girl, I know you've got your hands full, but do you think you could?"

Rachel stopped and gave Susan a hug. "I can't think of any way I'd be more happy and feel more capable to help you. I'm grateful for the opportunity. I love you, Susan. We are going to get you into the best, most progressive trial in the world," Rachel said. "How far are you willing to travel?"

"Mars, sweetie," Susan said grabbing Rachel's hand. "Let's pray?"

***

Taking a break from researching a new cancer study in Germany, Rachel stretched and looked at her phone. It was 9 p.m. and she still hadn't heard from Cody. She knew he had an important dinner with the man literally giving him a home in Manhattan for three months, so she couldn't be too put out. She had plenty of client dinners and the like back in her days as a lawyer and was familiar with the need to sort of roll with the evening, but she was feeling incredibly disconnected from him; and she didn't like it.

Since making the decision to live apart four days out of the week, Rachel had not allowed herself to think anymore about Cody's odd behavior when accepting the job offer. Everything about it had given her an icky feeling, but she didn't know why, so she didn't want to allow herself to pursue it. Now, sitting and waiting for him to call, feeling very alone, and totally consumed with all of the anecdotal cancer stories she had stumbled upon while doing clinical trial research, her brain was pulling it up — whether she wanted to or not.

Staring at her computer screen she replayed the portion of the call she had overheard...Cody taking the job and then getting obviously uncomfortable when asked to go to dinner on Friday. Then his not sleeping and the Bible verse he had referenced for support. It all added up to him walking into a situation he wasn't comfortable with.

It didn't make sense, Rachel thought. Cody was one of the most grounded, honorable people she knew. Those were the qualities she loved most about him...and she loved a lot of things about him. He was the type of guy to walk out the room, cover his ears, or bury his head in his phone if a movie scene got too steamy or the language got too vulgar, because he felt it chased away Holy Spirit. She would trust him in any situation. But, it made her wonder if he had stepped into a situation that he didn't trust himself.

Suddenly the name Simone came to mind. It bothered her. The name sounded French, sexy, *dangerous*. Rachel laughed at herself.

"You're being ridiculous," she whispered. "Go to bed. Read a book. You can talk to Cody in the morning."

She stared at the blinking cursor and then began typing in new search terms. *Cody Brooks and Simone. Cody Brooks and Simone and Stanford.* Before long, Rachel found herself staring at a handful of images from college Greek websites and *The Stanford Daily* student newspaper of Cody standing next to a beautiful girl with a sandy blond bob and a melancholy smile.

Simone Dumas.

Rachel despised the way the name sounded in her head. *Simone Dumas.* She sounded like a French siren who sipped espresso and smoked cigarettes, but smelled like roses and honey. A blend of seductive and sweet, dangerous and blameless. Reviewing the various images, Rachel could tell they were from different events, days, and times.

It looked like Cody and Simone had been more than just acquaintances or classmates. From what Rachel could surmise, they were good friends or dating. The discovery on its own was innocent, but the implications had Rachel's head feeling like it was going to explode. Why had he lied to make it sound like they barely knew one another? Why hadn't he approached Rachel to make sure she was comfortable with him working with an old girlfriend? The whole thing was building in Rachel's mind and she felt powerless to stop it.

*Stop. Take a breath*, a still small voice came from her heart. The gentle, loving whisper caught her attention amidst all the shouting in her head. She did as she was told. After three deep breaths, the noise subsided and she took a more rational look at the situation.

"Okay," she told herself. "You've played out the worst-case scenario. Let's think about the most innocent version of this story."

Cody had never lied about anything. It wasn't in his nature to lie or be manipulative. There had to be an explanation. None of the images online showed that he and Simone were anything more than at the same place, at the same time. It was very possible that engineering majors were invited to attend the pictured events and the two of them ended up close to each other because they recognized one another. Maybe she really is French and didn't speak very good English. Cody always had one-off, outsider-type friends because of his welcoming, compassionate disposition. If she appeared to be sad or lonely in anyway, Cody would have tried to be nice and befriend her.

After looking at both fabricated tales in her head, Rachel calmed substantially. There was probably a truth somewhere in the middle. Plus, she knew in her heart she trusted Cody completely.

While she didn't like that Simone was so pretty, or that she was getting to see Cody more than Rachel and the kids these days, she was sure the relationship was purely professional. Now that she had cooled her nerves, she was actually feeling a little sneaky and regretful for looking into it. She couldn't bring it up with him. It would look like she didn't trust him.

Rachel jumped as her phone suddenly rang.

Feeling like she had been caught with her hand in the cookie jar, she quickly picked up the phone.

"Hey," she said. "I was wondering when I'd hear from you."

"Hi," Cody answered, sounding tired. "Sorry I'm so late. I missed the kids, right?"

"Yeah, they're both asleep. How was dinner?"

"Good, fine. I don't know...good? Gary has asked me to consider taking on some additional responsibility once we get through this reporting stage."

"Really?" Rachel asked, concerned.

"Yeah," Cody breathed, sounding conflicted. "It's like a big deal. Totally flattering, but it's most likely going to prolong this needing to be on-site thing. We have some time to think about it, but we may want to talk about making a short-term move to the city. I won't do this living apart thing for much longer."

Rachel smiled. At least they were all on the same page with something.

"Wow," she said. "That's incredible you've already made such an impression."

"I guess," he said. "I'm not sure what to think. This city is totally foreign to me. It doesn't feel like home. But, I'm realizing very quickly the connections I'm making are setting us up to be successful *here*; not Collinsville."

***

It was now Rachel's turn for insomnia. Staring at the ceiling, her mind bounced back and forth between Cody alone in Manhattan with a pretty, old college friend, to the idea of moving the family to the city. Even more than the late night, anxiety-fueled fears of Cody rekindling a relationship with an old friend, Rachel worried about raising Slater and Skylark in a revised version of her youth. Would a childhood in New York City mean the same thing for them that it had for her?

She replayed the hot summer nights in the city when she was just 6 years old. The fights between her parents rivaled the heat in ferocity and drove Rachel out onto the fire escape for fresh air and solitude. She thought about her dad leaving, disappearing until just a year or so ago. And, she thought about the incredible afternoons she would spend with her mom walking through Central Park, going to see special screenings of *Breakfast at Tiffany's* and then walking by the actual location just off Lexington Avenue.

There was something magical about the city...but it also had a dark side. Her mind turned to her past life with Tom. The absence of Holy Spirit and the superficial excess of their time together left her feeling empty even in retrospect. But, *the views* she remembered. The views from their fancy penthouse apartment were spectacular and made Rachel feel accomplished, even if it was Tom's parents who had funded the bulk of the home.

Grabbing her pillow, she tossed it over her face and let out a small yelp. She needed to sleep. *She needed to pray,* she realized. Kicking her legs out from underneath the sheets, she kneeled down onto the floor next to her bed.

"Dear Heavenly Father, thank you so much for your continual guidance and love. I am so grateful for the many blessings you've given our family. There are a few things weighing on me though, Lord. I'm praying that you'll bless me with clarity in order to make good decisions for all of us. It seems like Cody's too caught up in doing a good job and it's up to me to review our situation objectively...please help me to be objective. His job in Manhattan seems a little questionable right now, as though we rushed into something without getting the whole story. But, we both thought it was divinely guided, so I don't want to disregard that. It doesn't feel right living apart the majority of the week; but I'm not sure it feels right moving our little family to the city. Please bless me with inspiration and help me to act with love and compassion. Don't let me get caught up in any of the unfounded emotions I'm having about Simone. And, please help there to not be anything to be concerned with there. Thank you, again, Lord. I love you. In Jesus' name, Amen."

Feeling lighter, sleepy, Rachel climbed back into bed and rolled on her side. Her arm lay out before her onto Cody's side of the bed. She stroked the sheet and his pillow, wishing he was there and soon drifted off to sleep.

***

The day was packed full of activities. A music class, playdate, and birthday dinner for Skylark. And, while such a schedule wouldn't have seemed like a big undertaking a year ago; today, it was quite an affair. Rachel had compiled a detailed itinerary to make sure they were able to accomplish everything, including naps, food breaks, some online cancer research and FaceTime with Cody.

Feeling slightly overwhelmed, Rachel tried to focus on just getting through breakfast. Slater rocked happily in his swing while she worked on making a picture perfect mini-stack of pancakes for Sky, who was still sleeping. Just as she heard the birthday girl waking over the monitor, she placed a pat of butter on top.

"Get ready to sing to your sister, I'll be right back," she said to Slater.

Running up the stairs, Rachel was greeted with a giant smile and nearly as big bedhead.

"Good morning, birthday girl!" she exclaimed, pulling her out of her crib and giving her a big hug and kiss. "You're one year old today. Can you believe it? Me neither."

Skylark looked at Rachel with her big brown eyes and smiled, realizing something special was happening. "Dada?" she asked...at least Rachel interpreted it as a question.

"No, sweetie. I'm sorry. No Dada. But, we get to talk to him in a little bit and he'll be home tomorrow when you wake up."

Suddenly Rachel could hear her phone ringing downstairs. "I think that might be daddy!" she said. "Let's go."

Rachel raced down with Skylark and grabbed her phone. Accepting the call she faced it at Skylark.

"Aw," Cody said. "There's my birthday girl. Good morning, love."

"You're timing is perfect," Rachel said. "I was just about to give Sky her breakfast."

Rachel placed Skylark in her highchair and positioned the phone on the table so that Cody could see. Then she grabbed the stack of pancakes, added a candle and brought it over.

"Happy birthday to you, happy birthday to you...," she sang, motioning for Cody to join in. "Happy birthday, dear Skylark. Happy birthday to you."

She smiled as she watched Skylark mesmerized by the flickering light of the candle.

"Okay, blow," she prompted.

Sky offered a soft, wide-mouthed huff. Rachel giggled and gently blew the candle for her. Clapping, she drizzled a little syrup on the stack and pulled out the candle.

Turning to Cody, she smiled. "So glad you called right now," she said. "I love that we both got to sing to her."

"I thought we weren't celebrating until Saturday," he said sounding slightly vexed.

"Well, we're not," Rachel said, trying to diffuse his dismay. "I just made her some pancakes. And, since it's *officially* her birthday, I didn't see any harm in acknowledging it."

She could tell he was irritated because he felt like he was missing out. Rachel hated how on-edge he was lately. The stress was already getting the best of them both. "I'm sorry if I made you feel like I was doing something without you," she added.

"No, no," he said. "You're right. Of course you should celebrate her today. I just hate not being there."

"We miss you. Glad you're home tonight."

"Dada!" Skylark added.

"Aw, sweetie," he said smiling at Sky. "I miss you ladies more than you know. Where's my boy?"

Rachel popped up and grabbed Slater from his swing and bounced him on her lap in front of the phone.

"Hey, buddy," Cody said. "How you doing with these girls? Wow. I swear he's grown since Sunday. He looks older, chubbier…more like a baby."

Rachel laughed. "As opposed to an infant?" she asked clarifying.

"Yeah. You know, he's losing that newborn look."

"Well, he eats all the time. It's good to know it's doing some good," she said. "You need to go?" She could hear the hotel room phone ringing in the background.

"In a minute," he said. "I'm meeting Gary and Simone downstairs for a working breakfast. We have to discuss the responsibilities falling under my new role and how I am going to implement the changes."

"New role?" Rachel asked, confused.

"Yeah," he said. "I was going to talk to you about it this weekend, but, like I mentioned, Gary's asked me to manage the renovations that I am recommending as part of my report. They've got me hiring a labor team to begin some of the work. I'm going to have to oversee them in addition to the work that I'm doing. I feel like I'm in over my head, but it's all great experience."

Rachel sighed. "I didn't know you were making any decisions yet. I thought you had more time," she said, confused. "So, this means you're going to be working on-site indefinitely?"

"We can talk about it this weekend," Cody said, making a face Rachel couldn't read.

"Okay," she said. "We love you."

"I love you all," he said. "Happy birthday, Sky. I'll be home tonight."

The screen went black and Rachel turned to her little children. "Well, you guys, what in the world are we going to do?"

Skylark was covered in pancake, happy as could be, and Slater was ready for breakfast.

"All right, you two, this is all on the itinerary. Sky, time for a birthday bath. Slater, you're going into the sling for breakfast."

While doing double duty, washing syrup out of Sky's hair and ears and feeding Slater virtually hands-free, Rachel contemplated the idea of Manhattan again. She just couldn't get her head around it. Beyond her own dual-sided childhood memories, she just believed Collinsville offered a better environment for raising her family. She agreed with Cody. He was building a resume for more work in the city. She knew if they compromised now and moved temporarily to Manhattan, it could very easily become permanent. She was not ready to give in yet.

\*\*\*

"Come in, come in," Rachel said giving Susan a hug. "Thank you for coming by. It's just more difficult these days to get out and about. We can sit in the living room while the kids play on the floor."

"Oh, girl. You have no idea how grateful I am. Plus, I'll take any opportunity I can get to see you and the littles. Truly a bright spot in my life."

As they got situated on the couch, Susan handed over a little gift for Skylark. "I know we're celebrating on Saturday, but I couldn't let her *real* birthday go by without a little something."

"Oh, Susan. Thank you."

Rachel pulled Skylark onto her lap and helped her open the sweet little teddy bear. Sky looked at it with big, excited eyes. She happily hugged it and bestowed numerous kisses on the plush toy's head.

"I haven't gotten such a great reaction ever to a gift, girl!" Susan exclaimed with a big laugh. "You know how to open up Auntie Susan's pocketbook."

"Lucky girl," Rachel said with a giggle, setting Sky down to play with her new teddy. "Okay, so let's talk."

"Go," Susan agreed. "I can't wait to hear what you've found."

"I still have lots of research to do; especially about how to apply and join these studies, but I've tracked down a couple of really interesting studies. There's one in Germany, one in China, and one right here in New York. Well, in Manhattan."

"Really?" Susan asked, curious. "Are they all pretty similar? I mean, I'd love a trip to Europe, but I'd prefer to go once I'm all healthy. The one in New York would be ideal, right?"

"Well, they're all really interesting, but there are some differences. Like I said, I need to look into them more, but they all have some real promise. For example, the one in China has already gone through a number of trials and the results are proving to be groundbreaking in stopping cancer."

"China!" Susan said in awe. "Could you imagine? What a trip. I think it would be hard to be somewhere so foreign while undergoing medical treatment...but, what stories I'd return with, right?"

Rachel laughed and gave Susan a hug. She loved her positivity. Even in the midst of such a challenging time, she just beamed with light and love.

"You would definitely have an enthralled audience at our Sunday potlucks," Rachel agreed. "The China study is not specifically focused on breast cancer though, it's looking at all types of cancers and basically they've discovered a way to just stop the cancer cells from multiplying. It doesn't shrink it, or get rid of it. It just stops it from growing or wreaking havoc — which is amazing and good to know."

"Interesting," Susan said. "I like having that in our back pocket if we can't find a study able to more aggressively just get rid of it. Of course, beggars can't be choosers."

"Susan," Rachel admonished sweetly. "You have every right to be as choosy as you want. You are going to review all of these and determine exactly which one you feel is best for you...and I'm going to get you in. The end."

Susan looked Rachel in the eye and Rachel noted an almost imperceptible quiver of her lip.

"I believe you," she said.

Rachel nodded. "Okay then. Germany's in the very early stages, but the trials are testing a new drug that's hoping to actually put healthy cells in overdrive to eradicate cancer cells. I don't fully understand it, but it sounds like it turns healthy cells into little Pac-Man's."

"Oh, I like the sound of that," Susan said with a smile as she knelt onto the floor to play with Skylark. "It feels like I have uninvited guests inside. I like the idea of little superhero cells eating them up."

Rachel found herself getting angry at the cancer as if it were a terrible person. She wanted the ability to kick them out, too. "I'm so sorry, Susan. I love you. I hate that you're having to go through this."

Susan patted Rachel's leg from the floor. "Girl, we've all got challenges. Holy Spirit is with me, helping me through. I feel so blessed to know Him and to be in this with His love and guidance. I can't imagine going through this without that knowledge, you know? I know I'm going to get through this. But, it does feel like my body has betrayed me a little bit," she said with a sigh. "What about the trial in New York?"

"The one in New York is also in early trials, testing a new drug, and is specifically focused on breast cancer, but I need to find out more."

"Well, I like that," Susan said. "Focused specifically on breast cancer is good. And, in early trials seems like it would be easier to get included, right?"

"I'll get more details," Rachel said determined.

"Rachel. Thank you," Susan said giving her a hug. "I'm so grateful to have you to help me with this."

Rachel squeezed her tightly. "I'm so, so happy to be able to help."

"I hate to be in and out, but I actually need to be on my way soon for a doctor's appointment. We're setting up my first Chemo treatment," Susan said, sticking out her tongue in disgust.

Rachel's heart dropped. There was something about the mention of Chemo that made it even more real. More urgent.

"When do you think they'll start?" she asked.

"I'm not sure. Soon, I think."

"Let me know as soon as you do. Some of the ladies and I are going to bring dinners over. Just so you don't have to worry about it," Rachel said.

Susan gave Rachel another hug. "Thank you, girl. Really. Thank you," she said patting her hand as she prepared to leave. "Does Cody come home tonight?"

"Yes, thank goodness," Rachel said.

Susan offered an understanding nod. "Can I take the kids for a couple of hours tomorrow?" she asked. "There's nothing I'd like to do more while I still have the energy. I'm sure Cody's dying to get some time with them, but I feel compelled to force you two on a date."

Rachel couldn't believe that she hadn't thought of it first.

"*Compelled*, huh?" Rachel asked with a wink. "Susan, you're totally doing it again. Making me feel like the only one who matters. But, this seems like an answer to a prayer I hadn't quite yet prayed. I think I'll take you up on that offer."

# CHAPTER FOUR
## IN HIS HANDS

There was nothing sweeter than watching Cody with Skylark. Of course Rachel also cherished seeing him with Slater, but how he interacted with their baby girl was magical. His joy in making her smile and giggle was contagious and made Rachel's heart feel as though it could burst.

Welcoming the day with two cups of coffee and tired eyes, Rachel's soul felt at peace, which only highlighted how out of sorts she felt when Cody wasn't home. Working to suppress her conflicted feelings, she relished the moment.

Cody had arrived home even later than expected. Falling asleep on the couch trying to wait up, Rachel woke when she heard his key in the door and Slater waking for milk simultaneously. She had hoped to have a few moments to welcome him home and share her plans for an afternoon date, but by the time she got to the bedroom, he had already passed out — his business casual khakis still on. She did her best to make him comfortable and found herself missing his threadbare work denim and old scent of sawdust.

Today was off to a good start though. Cody had just announced his plan to start putting off the Friday workday until he got back to the city Sunday afternoon. So, they now had two official play days per week. Rachel was looking for an opportunity to tell him about their afternoon date, but didn't want to put a damper on his time with the kids.

"What do you want to do today?" he asked cheerfully.

"Well, I was thinking it might be fun to go to the park this morning, then, this afternoon, Susan is going to come by for a bit to watch the kids and let us go on a little date," Rachel said, holding her breath.

Cody looked up from the floor where he was playing with Sky. "Is she up for it?"

"Susan? Yes. It was actually her idea, but as soon as she offered I realized how nice it sounded to get an hour or two with you to myself. Is that okay?"

"Absolutely," he replied, surprising her. "I'll just have to get my baby-fill now."

Burying his head in Skylark's tummy he blew raspberries and pretended to eat her up. The room filled with giggles and Rachel couldn't help but laugh too.

***

"I feel like I'm forgetting something," Rachel said as she and Cody made their way out of the house. "I haven't left the house without the kids in a long time."

Cody pulled her into him and embraced her. "We've talked about this. You need to take time for yourself. It shouldn't just be a special occasion because Susan offered or because I'm home. It should be a regular thing."

"Well, I'm grateful you were okay leaving Slater and Sky for a bit. I felt bad taking away from family time to have time together alone," she said starting to walk.

"I've missed you so much, Rach," he said. "Every night I go to sleep thinking I can't do this for another day. I wake-up questioning whether the means justify the end. It just doesn't feel right being away from you or the kids."

"I know," Rachel agreed, grabbing his hand. "I feel like we rushed into it without really knowing all that it would entail. It's sort of taken on a life of its own. But, are you enjoying the work? Is it better than working on commissioned pieces in your own workshop?"

"The work is actually amazing," he said, a twinkle in his eye. "It's the only thing that keeps me pushing forward. I do enjoy it. I love building something from scratch, but this feels like I am doing something bigger. I'm helping to bring something old and broken-down back to its former grandeur. It's rewarding. And, if I'm being honest the paycheck definitely makes me feel more like the 'man of the house,'" he said using air quotes. "I know it doesn't matter. We're blessed. We've been given so much and we've never had to struggle financially. But, it's sort of a nice boost to my ego to be the one bringing home the bacon."

Rachel smiled. She wanted him to be happy. They had never discussed whether Rachel's slightly larger salary from *Cali's* bothered him. It all just went into the same bank account, so she assumed it didn't seem to make a difference. But, if it made him self-conscious, she wished they would have talked about it sooner.

Cody shrugged and continued, "I just don't know if my pride is a good enough justification to be putting us all through this stress. When I'm honest with myself, that's what it comes down to."

"I want you to have everything you want," she said. "There's no reason you should have to compromise on something like this that brings you joy. If you see yourself doing this work long term and finding fulfillment in the future, we need to adjust to accommodate that. I want Slater and Skylark to see that work is a good thing, something that's a positive aspect of life —not something that you or I go to begrudgingly just to pay the bills. Where I see us needing to adjust and reconsider is in how we approach our next round of decisions."

As they approached Main Street, the afternoon sun was strong and Rachel could see Cody wincing. She hoped it was from the bright light and not her opinion on the topic.

" I just want to take some time to evaluate and go into any new decisions eyes wide open. I want to understand what we're in for, what it will entail, so we're not put in a situation where we have to be reactive again. For example, if you're serious about this work and it is going to require you being in New York the majority of the time, we need to really consider what that means — not jump into a situation that we're viewing as temporary only to realize it's *our life*."

The words reverberated in her mouth, echoing in her heart. Cody looked at her as if the words were rattling around him too.

"This *is* our life," he said. "I feel like we've both sort of brushed that fact aside."

Rachel wasn't sure she understood his point.

"We've both been just gritting our teeth and working to get through," he added. "Get through until Thursday night. Get through until I don't have to be in the city quite as often. We haven't been paying attention to the fact that this is our life. This is the experience we're giving Sky and Slater in their first year. This is the life we're choosing to live right now."

He was right. Rachel had been completely living in the future. She felt like that was what she needed to do to get through the challenge of being without Cody, being overwhelmed, feeling out of control, but it was wasting the precious moments she had right in front of her.

"You nailed it," she said, a little startled. "This is exactly why I've been feeling so out of sorts and unsure of what to do next. I'm not connected to the here and now. I'm totally living for the future."

"I've been doing the same thing. I haven't seen another way to get through how hard it is to be away from you guys, but it's time to reevaluate." He paused and looked down Main Street. "Where did you want to go? *Cali's*? *Watson's*? The park?"

"Ooh. *Watson's*, please. I love *Cali's* new healthy offerings, but I need some good, old-fashioned, Collinsville frozen Cheesecake Yogurt."

Cody smiled and took her hand. "I'm glad we're on the same page."

***

After a short conversation with Watson and debating whether to stick with her usual order or something new, Cody and Rachel found a quiet seat outside.

"How's your Cherry Cheesecake Yogurt with graham cracker crumble and chocolate chips?" Cody asked, smirking.

Rachel blushed. "Delicious...like *always*."

"I don't know why you even consider getting something else," he said. "You love what you love."

"It's so true. I'm also sentimental. I love that I can taste the same thing I enjoyed so many times with Auntie Cali. How's yours? What'd you get?"

"It's the Rocky Road flavor. It's good, but I should have stuck with the Mud Pie," he said with a chuckle.

81

"So, what are you thinking we should do? How do we fix this without ruining your opportunity to continue forward?" she asked.

Cody coughed and looked as though he had choked on his Cheesecake Yogurt. "Well," he said, stalling. "I'm not sure. The easiest solution seems to be move to Manhattan, but I have absolutely no idea how you feel about that. I have no idea how I feel about it, really."

Rachel nodded. "It's been on my mind and having been raised in the city, I'm not sure it's the life I want for Slater and Sky. I'm not sure it's the lifestyle I want for you or me, either. As you're discovering, it's different. Not bad by any means, just really different. Things move faster. Kids grow up faster. I appreciate the life we have in Collinsville."

She took a bite of her yogurt and thought for a moment.

"Even before we reconnected, I chose Collinsville to make my home. This place is special. It's filled with love, community, beauty, and...Him. You can feel Holy Spirit's presence here. It's shameful that I'm only now thinking about this, but maybe that's the problem."

"What?" Cody asked not quite following.

"Well, maybe we've lost sight of what our absolute focus should be...and by getting caught up in worldly things and seeking more, we're getting sucked into more worldly issues? Not sure I'm explaining it very well."

Cody took her hand in his. "Now, I think you've nailed it. I've been struggling with some version of that thought since I started. I'd felt like I'd been drawn into an unprotected space, as though I'm open to negative...I don't know...*things*."

Rachel shuddered.

"What do we do?" she asked. "I respect that you like the work, but I don't like that you feel as though you're in a bad situation."

"It's not a bad situation," Cody said, backtracking. "That's not really what I meant. It's hard to describe. I think it mainly has to do with being pulled out of my element. As well as being in a big, bustling place like NY. That's probably it more than anything. Daily I'm exposed to things that in Collinsville I never see."

"Exactly," Rachel agreed. "That's the stuff I'd like to protect the kids from. I appreciate that we aren't in a city apartment where you hear any song someone decides to blare on the street and that our park doesn't also double as a place for illicit interactions."

Cody looked sad. "That wasn't totally where I was heading with the conversation. There's also some good in being exposed to the world and not being somewhere so sheltered."

"Sure," Rachel said. "But, I'd prefer it in small doses."

"We're back to square one," he said. "I didn't intend to bring stuff up that would turn you off to the city. I was hoping to have you guys join me this week to feel it out."

"Oh, Cody. Nothing you said changed what I was already thinking. I know Manhattan well, remember? If living there is the only way to make you happy, we'll find a way to make it work. But, I would like to see if there are other options first. It's been less than a month, let's see how you feel about the city in a few more weeks…"

Rachel pushed her yogurt away, feeling a little nauseous all of the sudden. "This is going to sound like I'm not willing to compromise, but it's not the case at all. For now, I think it's really important to maintain the kids' schedule. It'll be too disruptive to just come out to the hotel room with you for a couple of days. The amount of stuff we'd need to bring just to make them comfortable would be crazy and I imagine it would still throw them off. If moving to the city is the only option. I'll do it. But, it'll be a move, not a trial run."

Rachel felt like a jerk. It was the first time she'd put the kids' needs before their own. Of course she wanted to go hang out with him in the city. If it were just her, it would be a blast to go relax in a plush hotel room, sightsee, visit her old stomping grounds, and see Cody's work; but it wasn't just her, and taking two babies to Manhattan and trying to keep them entertained, fed, safe, and on a decent sleep schedule, was a logistical nightmare.

Cody's eyes met hers and he smiled apologetically. "You're right. I'm totally thinking about my own comfort and it's not fair. It's my own selfishness that's gotten us here in the first place. Let's keep doing what we're doing for now. We'll get through the summer. By September my role onsite should be winding down and I'll be home more."

"Cody, you're not being selfish. I know you've been looking for an opportunity like this for a long time. The circumstances are just hard. We need to get creative and come up with a solution that'll work for our family."

"Yeah, I'll start talking to Gary about projects in Upstate…make it clear that I'd like to avoid more projects in the city," Cody said. "If I do that maybe some of the pressure from both him and Simone to do dinner and talk about city collaborations will ease up."

"Don't do anything until we've decided what we're doing together," Rachel said, annoyed that Simone played such a big role in his work. "Let's figure it out before you give anything definitive to your work."

She hesitated saying a thought that popped into her mind. Trying to bite her tongue, it began to grow and she felt as though she couldn't contain it.

"I just don't want to have something else happen, like what happened this week," she started, feeling remorseful as the words spilled from her mouth. "I know you felt pressure to take on the additional role, but you moved forward without confirming with me. I thought we were going to take a little time to discuss and decide. Then, mere hours later, I find out that you've accepted the role. By the way, I'd love to get a better idea of what you're doing, because really it sounds like a promotion...we should be celebrating you; but it's also increasing the amount of time you'll need to be in the city... and that...stinks."

Cody looked surprised and tired simultaneously. If she was being honest, the discussion was exhausting her too. It wasn't the date she had in mind, but it was a necessary conversation.

"I'm sorry," she added. "I really didn't mean to bring it up like that. I was just surprised by the decision and intended to talk to you about it at some point."

Cody shook his head. "Rach, I'm good at what I do. I know woodwork. I'm passionate about Arts and Craft style. I'm setting this project up for restoration success. But, with all that said, I struggle as a businessman. I think that's why I haven't maintained a steady flow of clients as a carpenter and craftsman. I'm not comfortable as a salesman in the slow times and when it's busy, I have trouble saying, 'No.' Simone called right after I spoke with you and gave me this whole spiel about how it was the best decision I could make for my career and for the family. I was crazy if I didn't take on the additional role. She made such a strong argument, I felt like I'd be stupid to say, 'No;' like it was the obvious choice."

Rachel recoiled a bit. She didn't understand why it seemed this woman was pursuing Cody. *It's all in my head*, she told herself. Something just wasn't jibing though.

"Why'd she care? What's in it for her?" Rachel asked.

Then, trying to tone it back, she added, "It just seems odd that she would call you so late, so soon after the opportunity had been presented to coerce you to take it, right?"

"I don't know," Cody said. "I think me managing that portion of the project will take some work off of her plate. So, she was probably eager to get me to sign on. Really, I'm not sure. She acts like we're buddies, so maybe she honestly thought it was the best move for my career and it was just a friendly gesture. Regardless, you're right. I should've held off and discussed it with you. I won't say anything or make any other commitments without talking it out with you first."

He stood and took their empty yogurt cups to the trash. Taking her hand, he pulled her in and gave her a gentle kiss, then embraced her in a big hug.

"I look forward to the day that we're able to just talk about the weather," he said. "It seems we're always in the midst of some heart wrenching challenge. Let's plan a Hawaiian vacation for October or something."

"Deal...well, as long as Susan doesn't need me at that point," Rachel said resting her head against his chest. "Can we go sit under a tree for 15 minutes? I'd like to sneak in a little cuddle time."

***

The backyard was bursting with streamers, balloons, and goodies. It seemed everyone who had offered to bring a side had also brought some adorable pink treat. The tables were covered with cake pops, cookies, mini cupcakes, and, of course, Skylark's birthday cake. Rachel had run upstairs to grab a lighter, but found herself drawn to the window, watching the festivities from above.

She mused, contemplating if this was similar to the view her mom and Aunt Cali had. She also wondered if celebrations would forever be bittersweet because they made Rachel miss them terribly. With all her heart she wished she could see what her mom would do for Skylark's first birthday. What lengths she would go to, to make it the most over-the-top princess party. She could see her mom covered in flour, face still flawless, whipping up a feast of delectable home-baked treats. While Cali would be cranking up the music and dancing like a gypsy, Skylark in her arms giggling and trying to catch one of Cali's wild bangle bracelets.

Rachel's heart dropped.

"Dear Lord, I can't lose another...*mom*," she whispered.

The deep-seated fear of losing another maternal figure in her life was too much to consider. Her sadness over losing her mom and then Aunt Cali at such a young age, almost did her in. Both times Holy Spirit was there to offer comfort and peace, but Rachel found herself wondering why it had to be that way in the first place.

"Why these beautiful, kind, *Godly* women?" she asked softly. "Why Susan? Why another woman who means the world to me? I'm not ungrateful, Lord, for all that you have given me. I'm blessed for the time I've had with each of these women...it's just...it doesn't feel fair. I'm sorry, Lord. Just please be with me. Help guide my research. Enable me to find the right clinical trial for Susan and please allow her to get the help that she needs to be healed. Please heal her, Lord."

Rachel took a deep breath and looked at herself in the mirror. After dabbing away a few tears and cleaning up her mascara, she made her way downstairs.

Looking around, Rachel couldn't help but reminisce about where life had taken them over the past year. She was grateful for so much. Most notably, because that time in her life was over. No matter how challenging things were now, the heartache and stress of everything they went through trying to legally adopt Skylark was worse. They could get through this. She and Cody could do this. They just needed to be present, think, come up with a thoughtful solution and be engaged for both Sky and Slater.

As she stepped outside, ready to head over and light the birthday cake, she noticed Cody off to the corner of the yard on his cell phone. He would never take a call during a family event like this, unless it was work.

Rachel felt a warm rush of anger flood through her veins, turning her cheeks pink and making her hands shake. Instantly she assumed it was Simone. If she considered herself Cody's buddy, it made sense that she would find nothing wrong calling to talk shop over the weekend…on one of the only full days he has with his family…during his daughter's first birthday party.

Susan walked over, smiling like the sun, with Skylark in her arms.

"Are we going to S-I-N-G, now?" she asked covering Sky's ears.

Rachel shrugged, struggling to hide her emotion.

"No, let's give Cody a minute. It looks like work has called."

"Got it," Susan said, raising an eyebrow. "Not very thoughtful of them to call on a Saturday, huh?"

Rachel knew Susan was picking up on her uneasiness. "Nope, it wasn't thoughtful. I just hope that it's a *thoughtless* oversight and not a calculated choice," Rachel blurted out.

"Oh, honey, why what's going on?"

"Nothing's going on," Rachel sighed. "I'm being petty. One of Cody's direct reports is an old college friend and I recently discovered she's a stunning, sophisticated, creative director named Simone. I'm pretty sure she's also French and probably has a sexy accent — at least that was what my imagination has convinced me of."

Susan smiled, her big cheshire grin. "You think Cody's being pursued by a French seductress?"

"Am I being ridiculous? I feel like being apart from him and spending so much time with two babies has me a little loopy."

"No, girl!" Susan exclaimed. "I'd never say you're being ridiculous. If you're sensing something's off…if your intuition is making you suspect something, listen to it. I wouldn't go accusing Cody of anything, because he may not even be tuned into it. But, intuition is a powerful thing. Just listen to your gut and pay attention."

Rachel was surprised by Susan's answer. She wasn't sure if it made her feel better or worse. She was happy her jealously, that she considered trifling, might have *some* merit, but she was also terrified that there might actually be *something* to her fear.

"You think?" she asked.

"Sure," Susan replied. "If you sense something is off, it's probably off. Although, it may not be in the way you suspect. It's just a little flag for you to pay attention to."

"Jeeze," Rachel said. "I don't have time for this. There's too much else going on."

Susan laughed. "Don't let it stress you out. Like I said, it could be nothing like what you think. Just don't ignore it."

Rachel took Skylark from Susan and went to get her dad and Slater. Just as she finished rounding up the bunch, Cody jogged over to join the group. Taking the lighter, he lit the singular candle on Skylark's cake and everyone sang Happy Birthday. Skylark couldn't get enough. Now, familiar with the song, she clapped along happily and blew out her candle like a pro.

***

Braiding her hair at the vanity before bed, Rachel had a flashback of her mom doing the same thing. First Sarah would do Rachel's hair. Getting it into a perfect French braid, they would listen to Frank Sinatra and talk about their day. Once Rachel's hair was done, Sarah would take a seat and let her hair out of whatever immaculate updo she had chosen that day. Typically in a chignon, her blonde hair would tumble down over her shoulders. Rachel would stand behind her and lovingly brush it, giggling any time she flipped it too fast, causing it to tickle her face.

She missed her mom. Fourteen was too young to lose her. She silently prayed that Skylark would fare better.

Staring into the mirror, but only seeing the visions in her head, she was frightened when Cody jumped into view surprising her from behind.

"Hey, beautiful," he said giving her a kiss on the cheek. "The party was a success. I think everyone had a great time, most notably Sky. She is passed out cold."

"I'm glad," Rachel said dreamily. "I'm tired, too."

She finished her hair and stood to give Cody a hug.

"Sorry I had to take that work call today," he said.

Rachel tensed. She had forgotten about it, but with Cody's mention the flood of irritation returned.

"It's okay," she said, feeling like she was being untrue to herself, but unsure of what else to say. "Was it very important?"

Cody shrugged. "I assumed it was, I couldn't imagine why else they'd be calling on the weekend. That's why I answered. But, it wasn't. They just wanted to connect about some of the things we're meeting about Monday," he said, waiving it off. "I got off as quickly as I could without being rude. I'll let them go to voicemail in the future...our time is too precious together."

"Sounds like a plan to me," she said, happy he felt the same way she did. But, she couldn't help but wonder who exactly "they" were. Why wasn't he ascribing a name to *them*? On one hand, he seemed removed, as though the people at work were the ones keeping him from his family, so he sort of clumped them all into one. On the other hand, was it really more than one person calling him to check-in about Monday, on a Saturday? Or was it *one* person calling to chitchat? *Just leave it alone*, she told herself. *Pay attention, but let it be.*

*\*\*\**

Lying on her belly, reading a book with Sky and Slater, Rachel felt a weight in the room. Saying good-bye to Cody always left such a gray cloud. Sky tossed her toy bear aggressively, Slater fussed, and Rachel flipped the book over to look at the cover.

"This book's sad," she said putting it down. "It shouldn't be made for babies. Let's have some fun, guys. We have a couple of hours until people start to arrive for the Sunday potluck. Let's have a dance party and then head to *Cali's* for a treat?"

91

Both children stared at her, eager for what was to happen next. Rachel leapt to her feet, turned on the stereo and began to hop around like she was a crazy person. She felt a little bit nuts, but she had to admit it felt good to let loose.

Skylark quickly followed suit and waddled around in circles, slapping her hands together in something that resembled a clap, occasionally stopping to bend over into a dance version of downward dog. Rachel lifted Slater into her arms and swayed with him. He instantly seemed happier, too.

"This is good, guys!" she exclaimed. "We need more dance parties in our lives!"

After a few minutes, they all relaxed and the mood in their home felt elevated. Rachel grabbed the diaper bag and secured both kids into the stroller and headed out the door. The excitement of upbeat music, and now, the fresh air, combined to bring Rachel out of her funk quickly. She hoped the kids were feeling it too. They appeared to be. Skylark continued to wiggle as though the music was still playing in her mind and Slater drifted off to sleep.

Now, if she could get some conversation with a full-grown human, things might feel totally normal. Approaching *Cali's,* Rachel felt a wave of peace. A soft breeze blew past and she knew Holy Spirit was with her.

"Thank you, Father," she whispered, softly. "You're so good to us. We needed your Spirit. I'm so grateful."

Stepping into the cafe, the sound of busy chatter, ice clinking in cold drinks, coffee brewing, and inviting music playing, was perfect.

"Rachel!" Robbie, one of the barista's shouted. "So great to see you. What can we get you?"

She ordered a drink and looked around for Maddy, whom she hoped was working.

"Is Maddy here?"

"She's out sick today," Robbie said. "But Susan Bishop's here. She's in the boutique."

Rachel's heart leapt. She hadn't gotten a chance to find out when Susan's chemo treatments were starting. Yesterday at Sky's party, Rachel was selfishly focused on Cody's work call. And, at church this morning Susan was busy being the gracious pastor's wife that she is. Grabbing her drink, she maneuvered her way with the stroller over to the boutique.

"Susan!" Rachel exclaimed. "Look at me, I'm out of the house like a normal person. I'm so glad to run into you. We didn't get enough of a chance to catch up at the party yesterday."

Susan smiled brightly, but Rachel could tell something was wrong.

"Is everything okay?" she asked.

Susan gave Rachel a hug and bent down to give Skylark a kiss on the head.

"Ooh, I want to kiss Slater too, but I'll let him sleep. " she cooed. "So good to see you, girl. Can you tell I'm a mess of nerves?"

"No, you seem as cool a cucumber," Rachel said. "I do sense something's bugging you though. What're you nervous about?"

"I start chemo tomorrow morning," she said sticking out her tongue in disgust.

"Really?" Rachel asked shocked. For some reason she thought she'd be kept more in the loop. She was grateful to be learning this news before it happened; but was sad it was during a happenstance meeting at *Cali's*.

"Susan, I'm here for you, always. Please don't ever hesitate to reach out when you're feeling down or nervous, or just want to talk things out. You might have to deal with some cranky babies in the mix, but I really want to be part of this journey with you, whenever you need me."

Susan smiled seemingly to hold back her emotions and gave her a hug.

Rachel suddenly felt prompted to continue. "I hope this isn't out of line, because I know Pastor Bishop's right by your side through all of this. But, I know you. You adore him. I see the way you touch up your lipstick before you're going to see him. I also see the way you nurture and cater to him. I'm sure you're worried about not being able to care for him when you're not feeling well. You're so selfless. Please, whenever you're feeling like you need help, whether it's making him dinner or getting you dolled-up when you don't have the energy — please text me. I know this is going to be a shift for you guys. And, you're in luck, my husband's gone, so I've got plenty of domestic free time."

Tears streamed down Susan's cheeks and she struggled to find her voice. In lieu of words, she gave Rachel a soft punch to the shoulder. "Darn you, girl," she whispered catching her breath. "You've made me ugly cry…in *public*. But, I love you for it. I love that you know me better than I know myself right now."

Rachel teared up as Susan worked to calm her tearful gasps. After a moment, she regained her composure. Dabbing at her eyes with a tissue, she said softly, "You're the Lord's hands on Earth right now, sweetie. Do you feel it? You just single-handedly answered every one of my secret prayers."

# CHAPTER FIVE
# MIXED EMOTIONS

Rachel was having a terrible time concentrating. With both kids asleep, she felt pressure to research cancer trials like she'd never researched before. But, every attempt to buckle-down and focus was preempted by competing thoughts. She found herself looking into everything from things to cook for chemo patients to how to raise Christian kids in Manhattan.

"Dear Lord, I need your help," she whispered. "I'm on limited time here. Please help calm my mind. Help me to get the squirrels out and focus on finding some good leads for Susan. Also, please be with her as she is going through her first treatment today."

Taking a deep breath, Rachel closed out the distracting secondary windows and returned to her search. Surprised, she found herself staring right at a recent news report from a business publication's website. The article interviewed a Long Island-based oncologist, Dr. James Hamming, whose unconventional methods had been yielding great results in a Phase 1 clinical trial for breast cancer patients with Invasive Lobular Carcinoma. Rachel gasped. *Just like Susan.*

Reading on, she discovered the trial, even though it had virtually eradicated the cancer cells in five of 20 participants, had been stopped because a patient had died. Until the cause of death was determined, the FDA had put the trial on hold, indefinitely.

"No," Rachel said.

Frantically, she began searching the US National Library of Medicine's database to find various medical journals with coverage of the study and its initial findings. The preclinical trials using non-human subjects had been just as promising, showing little negative side effects and impressive efficacy.

She found another news article from a community paper in Manhattan highlighting how the other participants were desperate to get the trial restarted. They didn't believe it was the test drug that killed their fellow participant. There were a number of conspiracy theories listed, which Rachel found unfortunate because it seemed to take away credibility from the people sounding the alarm. But, she could sympathize with their frustration. She was frustrated, too.

Just as she began to look into how to get a clinical trial re-opened, Slater woke.

"Okay, Dr. Hamming," she said shutting the computer. "I'll see you in a bit."

***

"We are not here for any other reason than to drop off dinner," Rachel said, carrying in bags of food from *Cali's* with Slater in the wrap on her chest and Skylark holding onto her leg. "And, I'm not going to even pretend that I made this. I offered detailed instructions, but I didn't make it. The potential for disaster is just too great these days... and while Cody and I can roll with it...you need nourishment, not burnt spaghetti."

Susan's eyes sparkled. Even though she looked tired, she still looked radiant and happy; which made Rachel happy.

"Thank you, sweetie," Susan said. "This is so thoughtful. I was afraid I'd be nauseous, but I'm feeling good. I'm sleepy. It's amazing how sitting all day can make you feel more tired than almost any physical activity."

Susan shrugged and rubbed Rachel's back happily. "I can't wait to dig into a beautiful, healthy *Cali's* kale salad, take a short bath, and go to bed."

Rachel laughed. "That sounds dreamy," she sighed quickly unpacking all of the food and putting it out nicely on the counter. "Okay, we're leaving now. Take care of yourself, relax, and call me whenever you feel like it. I'm eager to hear about your day, but when you are well-rested."

"Thank you again, Rachel. I'm so grateful for you."

Rachel ushered Skylark out the door and closed it behind them. Sky looked up at her mom, confused.

"Auntie Susan had a long day," she said picking her up. "We want to be helpful ninjas today. In and out, delivering yummy food and smiles. That's it. We'll get to spend more time with her another day."

Sky was already busy looking at her little brother, touching his lips and making him smile.

"Alright, you two, let's go home for FaceTime with dad, huh?"

***

Walking in the door, Rachel had a sinking feeling he was going to miss their scheduled call again. She shouldn't have brought it up with Sky, only because she never wanted her to feel let down. A feeling Rachel knew all too well from her childhood. Parallels between her childhood kept cropping up, and she wondered if it was her own paranoia or if Cody could ever possibly have some similarities with Joe.

The thought caused her to shudder. While she was grateful to have reconciled with her estranged father over the past two years, she still had a very grim view of what he must have been like as a husband. Her heart ached for her mom any time she relived some of her childhood memories from a married adult perspective. To think for even a moment that Cody could have some of the same characteristics, or be so unaware and self-absorbed, as Joe was crazy…*wasn't it?*

Rachel placed Slater in his swing, sat Sky in the playpen, turned on some fun music and got started making dinner. If he did call on time, she could breakaway; if he didn't, she and the kids wouldn't be hopelessly waiting around getting hungry and frustrated. This way Rachel could temper any disappointment she thought and then laughed at herself. Of course Skylark would enjoy talking to her Daddy on the phone, but did she have the awareness to even notice if it didn't happen? And, Slater. At this point the calls were just helping to ensure he had some level of recognition of Cody. Everything aside, Rachel was the only one experiencing disappointment and there was nothing she could do to temper it.

Looking at the clock, she shook her head realizing it was 30 minutes past their scheduled call time. She plated her and Skylark's dinner and brought everyone to the table. Getting situated with Slater, she fed him while they ate. Meals like this made her vacillate between utter awe and adoration of her children and feeling a bit less than human. Both children were amazing and being a mom was incredible, but a day filled with nothing but serving them from morning to night could leave her feeling drained and a little vulnerable. It was just hard not having someone else at the table to connect with, commiserate with.

After taking a couple of bites of pasta, Rachel switched Slater over to her other side, and looked at Skylark listlessly. Busily eating and playing in her highchair, Sky barely took notice.

"You know I'm not a fan of the T.V. at dinner, but mommy's going to put something on," she said, needing something to distract her for just a few minutes. "Let's watch something funny."

***

Rachel could see she had a missed call when she finally made it downstairs from getting the babies to bed. Looking at the clock it was nearly 9 p.m. *Why so late again*, she wondered. She listened to the voicemail.

"Hey, Rach," Cody's voice sounded apologetic. "Sorry to miss our scheduled time. I may need to get some pointers from you...from your days as a Manhattan lawyer...on how to say *no* to colleagues. I'm struggling with all of the extracurricular things the team asks me to. I don't know how to decline without coming off as self-important or uncompromising. Anyhow, I miss you guys and I'm sorry. Call when you can."

Rachel went to delete the call when she realized the little timeline showed nearly three minutes of additional recording. He must have not ended the call. Instantly her face became hot with self-consciousness and hesitation as she continued to listen in, wondering what else she might hear. She trusted him, she told herself. Listening to a voicemail, wondering if she might catch something, did not demonstrate that faith. Against her better judgement she continued to listen as she could hear him groan, sitting down on the bed, turning on the T.V., getting up, turning on the faucet in the bathroom.

She knew his routine from home. She could picture him in his hotel room, getting ready for bed, taking off his socks, washing his face, catching the news for the day. It made her miss him and realize he was in no better position than her. While the room in the city may have been novel for a minute, it sounded lonely. Even more lonely than her situation.

Suddenly, she could hear what sounded like a knock over the recording. The faucet shut off and she could hear Cody say, "What the heck?" After a pause, there was another knock and the T.V. went mute. "Just a minute," he said, apparently getting a shirt on.

Rachel's heart was pounding as though it was going to pump out of her chest.

She could hear him undo the door chain and unlock the door.

"Simone, what're you doing here?" Cody asked. Rachel felt she could discern a hint of annoyance in his voice.

"I'm so sorry to bother you," Simone seemed to reply. Rachel could barely hear her, but her stomach turned as she realized she did have a French accent.

"There's a strange man downstairs and he's made me rather uncomfortable," Simone continued, louder, more clearly, making Rachel wonder if she had stepped into the room. "I was hoping you might walk me out? Help me catch a cab?"

"Of course," Cody replied. "I just need to get my shoes on. Please take a seat."

Rachel could hear him sit on the bed, pull his shoes on and throw on a jacket.

The door opened and slammed shut, and all was silent. After a few more seconds the recording ended.

Rachel felt like a jerk for listening. Well, she felt awful for allowing herself to get worked up about it. It definitely wasn't an indication of complete and utter trust. The interaction was completely innocent and understandable. Rachel had found herself in a similar position years ago after a late work dinner when she lived in the city. Without someone like Cody at her beck and call, she ended up asking a stranger to help her to a cab.

*Let it go,* she told herself. But, *pay attention,* echoed in her mind. The words of Susan reminded her to be aware, so she decided to tuck the encounter away in a corner of her mind.

Staring at her phone, she debated whether or not to call Cody back. Her emotions had taken such a rollercoaster ride, she wasn't confident that she could be relaxed with him. Even with his complete innocence, Rachel inherently felt a little betrayed.

"Come on," she prodded herself. "He did nothing wrong. Plus, it sounds like he's had a tough night."

On the fourth ring, Rachel started to wonder if he had already gone to bed. Anticipating to leave a voicemail and head to bed herself, she was surprised when he picked up, apparently mid-sentence with someone else...a female, who was laughing in the background.

"Hi, Rach," he said, casually. "Hold on one sec."

Her face started to burn again. It had been at least 20 minutes since he left the voicemail, more than enough time to get Simone to a cab and for him to return to his room, alone. Rachel felt tempted to hang up, but worked to maintain her cool.

In the background she could hear Simone, "Thanks, again, my knight in shining armor. I truly appreciate your chivalry. See you in the morning."

"Oh, it was nothing, really," Cody replied.

Rachel heard what she thought was a kiss, putting her on the verge on screaming, and then a car door slam.

"Hi, Rach. I'm sorry. It's been a strange night."

"Oh yeah?" she said, attempting to play dumb through gritted teeth. "Why?"

"Well, I got swindled into doing another work dinner. These people apparently don't have anything else in their lives except work...or they're using the opportunity to write off nice dinners, I can't tell. But, I ended up at dinner with Simone, Gary, and a couple of his partners. It was an odd mix. The partners were from Japan and drank, a lot."

He exhaled loudly, a noise she had come to identify as deep frustration.

"Anyhow, their antics captured the attention of a number of people in the restaurant. Some other heavy drinkers decided we'd be a good group to taunt. Mind you, this is a super upscale steakhouse on the first floor of the hotel I'm staying in...not some dive bar. I'd never seen anything like it. I wasn't sure what to do. Luckily, Gary called it a night, got his partners in a cab off to their hotel, and we all headed out. Well, at least I thought we had."

"What do you mean?" Rachel asked.

"Right after I got up to my room," he said, lowering his voice as he walked through the hotel. "Someone knocks on my door. So, I go to the door to find it's Simone. I don't know why she didn't leave when everyone else did, but those guys were giving her a hard time and she wanted me to come down and help her get a cab. The whole thing felt a little odd. But, I take her downstairs and am suddenly confronted with these drunk guys. I've never been in a situation like that…which may sound strange to some guys, but I haven't. So, I, peace-loving and extremely sober, tried to reason with them — which went nowhere. But, as luck would have it, security arrived right before I had to decide whether to use Simone or my fists as a shield."

He laughed at his joke.

"Wow, what an eventful evening," Rachel said, relaxing slightly. "It's too bad that you're getting roped into things by association."

"Yeah," he agreed. "The whole thing made me run up to my room and hide."

Rachel laughed, because she believed it.

"And, that's what I love about you," she said. "Leave that worldly stuff to the world. It's hard enough trying to navigate this life with a clear conscience, sober mind, and God on your side, all of that other stuff just clouds everything. It makes me sad for people who haven't found the truth."

"Amen to that," Cody said, his hotel door closing. She could hear him lock and latch it. "How are the kids?"

"They're good. We had a good day. Went to the park, a music class, picked up dinner for Susan and Pastor Bishop from *Cali's*. She had her first chemo session today. She was there for like 8 hours. We just dropped off some food and left. She looked great as usual. I've found a clinical trial that would be perfect for her, but it's paused indefinitely. I feel like I might need to see if there's an opportunity to try and get it reopened. I don't know. I need to pray about it."

"I miss you guys," he said. "I'm to the point that I'm starting to miss other things, too. I miss Collinsville. I miss our barbecue. I miss the Sunday potlucks."

"We miss you," she said. "I miss you at the barbecue. So…did Simone get off okay?"

"Yeah, after security took care of the guys, I got her a cab and sent her off."

"That's good," Rachel said, still feeling a little worked up.

"I'm going to take a shower and go to bed," Cody said. "This whole night has me feeling gross. I'd forgotten, probably because it wasn't a big deal in college, but Simone kisses as a greeting. Like she gives little cheek kisses. When I put her in the cab tonight she gave me two kisses on the cheeks to say goodnight. The kisses alone invade my personal space, make me uncomfortable; but after she left, the doorman said something about how I shouldn't let a 'hottie like that go home alone.' The city, most of the people, are just different, you know? We're really sheltered in Collinsville, and I'm coming to appreciate that more and more each day."

Rachel's heart did a flip-flop. She was so grateful for Cody's transparency. She loved his honesty and innocence. She prayed the city didn't harden him. At the same time, she was totally disgusted that Simone was kissing him. Rachel understood it was the cultural norm in France, but in New York it was inching too far onto her turf.

"Yeah, your cheeks are for me, the kids, and little old ladies at church, only," she said with a laugh that she hoped sounded more good-natured than jealous.

"Sounds good to me," he said. "I'm just not sure how to stop her without offending her."

"I don't know, Cody. This whole situation makes it sound like you've moved to another country, or are on some other planet. You're dealing with things that are beyond being in the city. I mean, being there definitely exposes you to some worldly stuff, but you're in on a different level."

She hesitated for a moment. "Some of it's making me uncomfortable, honestly."

"Yeah, it's the people I'm working with," he agreed. "It's making me uncomfortable, too. But, I've got a big day tomorrow. I'm hiring my team to perform the renovations. There's a bunch of interviews lined up. I'm hoping to try and catch the kids in the morning, but then I'll be out of pocket the rest of the day."

"Wow, interviews?" Rachel asked.

"Yeah, it should be interesting…just more stuff to push me out of my comfort zone," he said with a sigh. "I love you. Make sure the kids know I love them, too."

"Love you."

***

"Hi, may I please speak with Dr. James Hamming?" Rachel asked.

"Are you a patient?"

"No," Rachel replied. "I represent a party interested in helping to reopen his Invasive Lobular Carcinoma clinical trial."

"One moment, please," the receptionist said.

Rachel held her breath awaiting her return.

"Ma'am?" she replied.

"Yes?"

"Dr. Hamming is open to meeting with you. Are you available Friday at 3 p.m.?"

Rachel hadn't considered an in-person meeting.

"Yes, of course. Where should I meet him?"

"At his office in Manhattan. Do you have a pen? I'll give you the address."

***

105

The irony was almost comical. Rachel couldn't believe she was up at 5 a.m. heading to the city, just eight hours after Cody returned home for the weekend. He had not been happy about the trip, but realized the importance. Although, when he asked her what her plan was and her response had been, 'not sure yet,' she could tell he thought it was a frivolous outing. Maybe it was, but Cody had never seen her argue a case (luckily she never had to with him). She believed she would make headway with whatever plan ended up coming together.

Tom had agreed to meet with her at his office at 9 a.m. to discuss tactics. Rachel figured two lawyers were better than one, even if neither of them specialized in healthcare or clinical trials.

As she backed out of the driveway, she said a prayer Cody and the kids would have a nice day together. No matter how disappointed she was to be losing another day as a family, her mission felt noble. The potential payoff outweighed the loss, which was better than she could say for Cody's job at the moment. She had yet to tell Susan about the trial or the trip to the city, so as not to get her hopes up.

Dressed in one of her old dress suits, she was happy it still fit after having Slater. The sleek tailoring and gray color made her feel strong and smart. While tying her hair up in a French twist prior to leaving, she wondered if it would be too confining to parent in such a professional ensemble — as long as she could move, she'd be a lot more confident.

***

As the city skyline surrounded her, her anxiousness began to kick in. The nerves, similar to what she used to experience prior to a big meeting or an important court preceding, were a good thing. A feeling she could harness and ride. She had forgotten how much she loved this stuff. Way too close to it

106

all when they were trying to figure out Skylark's adoption, now Rachel had the passion and the distance to really make an impact. She hoped.

She found a parking garage a block from Tom's office and put on her heels, made sure she had all of her research and made her way to a coffee shop to kill time.

"You're perpetually early," a voice came from behind as she waited in line for a coffee.

"And, would the alternative be better?" she asked turning around to greet Tom. "Isn't this Starbucks off course for you?"

"I'm less rigid these days. Sometimes I even switch my order entirely."

"Well, that calls for a drink," she said, giving him a side hug. "What can I get you?"

"Whatever you're having," he said. "Did you want to meet here? I can grab a table."

"That'd be great," she agreed, relieved she didn't have to go up to her old office.

Taking a seat with him at a little corner table, she reached into her bag to pull out her research.

"You know, we really need to stop meeting like this," Tom said, his signature smirk on his face.

Rachel was flustered when her stomach inadvertently flittered with butterflies.

"Um, yeah, I'm sorry to rope you into my stuff again," she stammered, wondering in her heart what in the world just happened.

"I'm just teasing. I like getting to see you every once in a while. Plus, I'm glad you still value my opinion."

"You're a good lawyer," she replied, regaining her composure. "Let me show you what I've found."

She placed a number of the articles she had discovered on Dr. James Hamming and his clinical trial on the table.

"My friend Susan was recently diagnosed with advanced stage Invasive Lobular Carcinoma of the breast, basically really bad breast cancer," Rachel said. "I've been spending any free time I have researching clinical trials. This was by far the most aggressive and efficacious, and it just happened to be focused on the exact type of cancer she has. In the beginning stages, it had already put a number of the participants in remission — which is unheard of. But, one of the participants died and even though there wasn't an immediate or direct link to the trial, the FDA stopped it indefinitely. My goal is to investigate why the participant died and make a case that their death had nothing to do with the trial, to lobby and get the trial re-opened. And, of course, get Susan entered."

"Sounds like a plan," he said. "How you have time for this with a kid, is pretty impressive. Where can I help?"

"Two," she said, softly. "I'd love to have your help in tracking down the participant's information."

"Two?" he asked surprised. "You adopted another already?"

"I gave birth to a boy 10 months after adopting. It wasn't expected, but it's been incredible."

"Impressive," he replied trying to sound casual, but Rachel could tell he was surprised. "I'd be happy to get the info for you. So, you're meeting with the doctor today? How'd you finagle that?"

"I told his assistant that I represent a party interested in helping get the trials restarted," she said, her cheeks turning red with the admission. "It's not a *total* lie, just a little one."

"It's semantics and it's getting your foot in the door," he said dryly. "You're good at this. You know you miss it. Do people in your little town even know what a star you were in the big city?"

His words pierced her gut. From the moment her Aunt Cali died and she chose to move her life to Collinsville, she hadn't allowed herself to even think about her former life as a lawyer, as Tom's girlfriend...almost his wife. But, she suddenly wondered if it was because she knew, deep down, she did miss it, there was a part of her that loved the high-profile, powerful role of a lawyer in Manhattan. The lifestyle it afforded and the drive it took to succeed everyday offered such immediate gratification.

"It's not who I am anymore," she replied, trying to rectify within herself why all of these shocking feelings were emerging. She had chosen to leave Tom, the job, the city and to embrace an existence more in line with her beliefs. She loved her pure, sweet life in Collinsville and every blessing that had come as a result of her being there.

"No, I get it," he replied. "You've chosen to live a more Christ-filled life. It can be challenging here. Especially with a negative influence like me...well, the old me."

"The old you?" she asked stumped.

"I've been inspired to make some changes, too," he said. After helping with Skylark's adoption case last year he had asked her a few questions about God and the Bible, but Rachel had almost forgotten.

"That's great," she replied. "Are you going to church?"

"I'm making changes slowly," he said with a wink. "Anyhow, you're an excellent lawyer. I just don't want to see you sell yourself short because you've chosen to be meek and humble. Look at all the good you could do."

Rachel slightly shrank at his assertion. There was definitely something misaligned in her mind about being a successful lawyer and Christ-like at the same time; the two didn't jibe. Today, she was going for strong and powerful. So, if he was seeing meek and humble, she needed to tighten her hairdo.

"Anyhow," he continued. "Your meeting with the doctor today will be a success no matter what angle you take. I'll see what I can track down on the dead guy. I have some time today, do you want me to go to the meeting with you?"

Rachel recalled how well they worked together. It was more likely than not the reason they stayed together as long as they did. Their research methods, personalities, and tactics complemented one another. With clients they balanced one another to both charm and impress. Independently, they were both smart, good lawyers; together they were brilliant.

"You want to go with me?" she asked suspiciously.

"Sure, it'll be like old times."

***

Rachel was 30 minutes early to the doctor's office. Finding a nice leather bench in the downstairs lobby, she plugged in her phone and reviewed her notes. Still a bit dazed by her morning meeting with Tom, she was grateful, yet on guard, for his willingness to help. She watched the revolving door vigilantly for any signs of him. After a few minutes she spotted him strutting through the lobby, she waved to grab his attention and grabbed her phone that had unexpectedly started to ring.

Assuming it was Cody, she picked-up without looking and continued to work to get Tom's attention.

"Hi?" she answered, distractedly, making eye contact with Tom and motioning for him to come take a seat with her.

"Ms. Brooks?" an unfamiliar man's voice came on the line.

"Yes, this is Rachel Brooks," she said, making a confused face at Tom.

"Dr. Hamming, here," the man said and Rachel mouthed to Tom, *it's the doctor.* "I wanted to call you myself to apologize. I'm not typically one to neglect my commitments, but I'm not going to be able to meet with you this afternoon. I've had a family emergency develop, my dear aunt is ill, and I've had to leave the city for the weekend. I apologize for any inconvenience this may cause. I'm still very interested in meeting with you, do you have time next week?"

Rachel's stomach turned, she wasn't keen on the idea of coming out to the city again next week; but this was important.

"Yes, of course, I completely understand. I hope your aunt is okay. Can I put you on hold for just a minute while I check my calendar for next week?"

"Sure, I'll hold," he said.

Rachel put her phone on mute and looked at Tom.

"He's cancelling. He had to leave early and wants to reschedule for next week."

She started to text her dad to see if he and Pam were available to watch the kids on Wednesday, so she could come into the city with them, take the meeting and leave without losing another day with Cody.

"I'm just going to see if he can meet on Wednesday next week," she said still looking at her phone. "I'm sorry to waste your time, Tom."

"Schedule it for 1 p.m.," he replied. "I have an opening."

"You really want to help with this?" she asked.

"Sure," he said, smirking again. Rachel averted her eyes. "This is way more exciting than real estate law."

# CHAPTER SIX
## REARVIEW MIRROR

Rachel shot up out of bed, disoriented and dazed. Taking a moment to regain her bearings, she realized Slater's cries had woken her from a deep sleep…and bizarre dreams. Grabbing her bathrobe, she quickly made her way down the hall. As she took him into her arms and settled in the rocking chair, a flood of dream fragments returned. Feeding her sweet baby boy, she drowsily tried to piece them together.

She recalled appearances from Cody, Susan, Aunt Cali, Simone, and Tom — at least twilight versions of them. The dreams had an air of otherworldly realism that had her questioning what was true and what wasn't. *Was Susan really better? Was there something actually going on between Cody and Simone? Had Aunt Cali returned to help with the kids?* Rachel closed her eyes to try to recapture the vision of her beautifully wild aunt walking through the door.

Bangle bracelets jingling, her blonde, long curls in a mane around her face, she had walked through the front door with a divine glow. Embracing Rachel in the warmest, most comforting hug, she had said, "Oh, honey, it's so good to see you. I told Jesus you really need me right now. He agreed. So, here I am. Now, where are those babes?"

Trying to feel the serenity of Aunt Cali's hug one more time, Rachel worked to replay the dream again and again. When suddenly her mind chose to move on to another snippet of dream featuring a sweet, simple kiss; a kiss with... *Tom.*

Rachel's eyes fluttered open and she tried to erase the memory. She felt disgusted by her own mind and wanted to reach into her head to scrub out the thought. She wondered what would work like elbow grease and Comet for the recesses of her brain.

*It's just a dream,* she thought, trying to calm herself down. *It doesn't mean anything. Maybe it represents something else? Maybe it's a memory from when you were together? You did used to kiss him, a lot.*

Looking at Slater, she could see Cody's handsome features and a wave of guilt hit her. Taking him back to his crib, she gently laid him down and took a deep breath. With all of the time apart, red flags from Simone, and her meeting with Tom, Rachel realized her emotions were a jumbled mess. Her dream had nothing to do with reality.

If her dream was real she'd be sitting with Aunt Cali right now, drinking coffee and getting the inside scoop on Heaven.

Determined to get back on track, Rachel vowed to make this Saturday all about the family, filled to the brim with togetherness and love. No distractions allowed. Slipping back into bed, she looked at the time: 5 a.m. She had another hour or so to sleep. Wrapping her arms around Cody, she put her cheek against his back and listened to the rhythm of his heartbeat and fell asleep to the soothing pulse.

***

Rachel had bacon and hash browns ready by the time Cody made it downstairs. She greeted him with a kiss and a cup of coffee as he sluggishly took a seat at the table.

113

"Man, all day with the kids wiped me out," he said with a laugh. "I'm sore. I guess I'm out of practice."

Rachel handed him the newspaper and poured pancake batter onto a hot skillet.

"How was it, though?" she asked. "We didn't get to talk much when I got home."

"Yeah, we were both a little zombie-like," he agreed. "Aside from you not being here, it was awesome. I love spending as much time as I can with them. I don't think you realize it, because you're with them everyday, but they change so much in a week. It's incredible how much they've both grown and learned since last Sunday. It makes me sad that I'm missing the day-to-day; but in a way it's making me hyperaware of the subtle changes."

"Keep track of that stuff, because I don't always see it."

She handed Cody a short stack of pancakes and wrapped her arm around him.

"I missed you so much this week," she said. "It took everything I had to leave yesterday knowing you were here."

"Was it worth it?" Cody asked.

His choice of words pained her. She knew what he meant, but it made her bitter that he would ask. She felt the desire to ask the exact same question every time he returned from the city, but she tried to refrain knowing it wouldn't make anything better.

"Well, I accomplished quite a bit," she replied, choosing her words carefully. "Which could mean a whole lot for Susan. But, I may have to go back to the city again next week."

"What?" Cody asked, visibly concerned.

"The doctor, Dr. Hamming, had to cancel last minute," Rachel admitted hesitantly. She didn't want to give Cody fodder or lead him to believe it wasn't worthwhile.

"We're rescheduling for Wednesday," she added. "While it was disappointing, my meeting with Tom was a success. He's looking into the deceased participant's information for me."

"How're you going to make Wednesday happen?" he asked.

Rachel noticed he had stopped eating his breakfast.

"Well, my dad and Pam are going to watch them. I'm going to have to head to the city in the morning, drop them off, go to the meeting then get them and head home. It would be ideal if you were able to breakaway for an hour or two to hang out with us."

"I'm sure I could get away for a bit," he said, something off in his voice. "Rach, I don't understand why you're so flexible now. Why you're willing to head to the city multiple times when you've been really firm telling me it wasn't in the best interest of the kids."

She looked at his face. He was sincerely hurt. He wasn't looking to pick a fight. And, now, confronted with his feelings, she agreed she had been extremely unyielding to his wishes. And, why? Was it because she was subconsciously angry at him for being in the city? Was she holding her fears and assertions about Simone against him? Or was it really not worth the kids' discomfort for a trip to the city?

She leaned into him and bent down to give him a kiss.

"Cody, I'm sorry," she said. "You're right. I haven't been very fair. I've made you do all the work, and realistically we probably could head to the city one day a week to visit you for lunch or something. But, it seems like a lot of work for the payoff. Right now, the trips make sense because I'm on the precipice of figuring out some really important stuff that could potentially save Susan's life."

Rachel suddenly got emotional.

"I'm sorry," she added. "I just can't lose another important woman in my life. I'm not going to the city to spite you or to be hypocritical, I'm sacrificing and putting the kids in an unideal situation because the potential payoff is worth it."

Cody wrapped his arms around her waist and put his head on her stomach.

"I get it," he said. "I'm sorry to give you a hard time. I just miss you guys so much. I'll be excited to see you on Wednesday. What time are you thinking?"

"My meeting is scheduled for 1 p.m., so I'm guessing it'll be around 4 p.m. Maybe we can do an early dinner?"

Skylark's morning chatter came across the baby monitor.

"I'll get her," Cody said eagerly.

When he returned, he had both kids in his strong arms. Rachel's heart melted. Giving Skylark a kiss, she took Slater and got ready to feed him.

"I want today to be all about family," she said sitting at the table. "I was thinking it might be fun to ditch the phones and just be totally focused on us. What do you think?"

"Sounds great to me," Cody agreed. "Here, take it."

He slid his phone across the table. Rachel put it on the sideboard.

"So, what's the plan?" he asked, curious. "What're we doing today?"

*** 

Everything smelled like earth and apples. It was delicious. Rachel took a deep breath and exhaled slowly. It couldn't be more picturesque. And, of course, without the phones, they weren't taking any pictures. She would have to tuck this away in her memory as a perfect day.

After some discussion, they had decided to drive a little further north to a well-known apple orchard. They'd spent the better part of the morning picking apples, drinking cider, and eating homemade concession stand food. Both kids lay full and asleep, sprawled out on the red and white checkered cloth she and Aunt Cali used for picnics when Rachel was a kid. She and Cody lounged next to them in the grass, talking and laughing like two young lovers. The dappled sunlight provided the perfect shade from the late summer afternoon heat.

"How can this feel even more bucolic than Collinsville?" Rachel asked with a laugh.

"Well, they have livestock and we've got Main Street," Cody said. "We're big city folks by comparison."

Rachel smiled and closed her eyes. "Big city," she repeated. "I don't want to think about the *big city*."

Cody touched her hands and she opened her eyes to look into his. He smiled, hesitantly, and Rachel's heart swooned.

"What is it?" she asked.

"You just said you don't want to think about it, but I was wondering if you have thought about it? I was just curious if your trip to the city made you feel any differently?"

"About moving to Manhattan?" Rachel asked. "Is that what you want to do?"

Cody shrugged and laid down to look at the sky. "I have no idea," he admitted. "I was just wondering. I don't want to be there alone anymore."

Rachel rested her head on his hip and looked at the kids.

"Let's give it some more time," she said. "We'll keep trying to make new concessions and figure out new ways to compensate, you know? It seems every week we come up with something else that makes it that much better. Like you pushing your Friday work to Sunday, or if everything works out Wednesday, a weekly trip to the city could be a possibility. And, a big one would be, making sure we prioritize scheduled FaceTime calls, even if you have a work dinner or we have something like helping Susan. Those calls should be non-negotiable."

Cody nodded.

"What do I do about those dinners anyway?" he asked. "They're seldom actually work dinners. They're social, but I feel obligated to go and maintain good standing."

"I had clients like that," Rachel recalled. "Those that wanted to meet up just to chat. I know that feeling of obligation. But, my dinners were maybe once a month. Your situation's different, because this is your daily job. These dinners are their social life it seems. They're doing it for fun and to build friendships. I don't see anything wrong with you either excusing yourself for a little while to do the calls with us; or skipping out altogether occasionally. Sure, I agree, you need to do the social thing with them, but not every time. Ultimately you need to figure out what you want to achieve through this job, you know? Also, you should consider whether these are friendships you want to cultivate. You're going above and beyond, but for what?"

Cody looked pensive and then closed his eyes, turning his face to a ray of sun. Skylark began to shift. Rachel felt her nerves tighten slightly. She wondered if Cody caught her drift about building relationships with his co-workers. Aside from Gary, they all sounded questionable — too caught up in things that weren't in alignment with Cody's values. Gary was only exempt because Rachel knew nothing about him except he was putting Cody up in one of his fancy hotels. And, Simone…well, whether Cody thought it was appropriate to build a relationship with her or not, Rachel was on high alert and hopeful that he would just outright tell her the after hours phone calls and meet ups were not appropriate.

"Hello, my sweet girl," Rachel cooed. "How was your nap?"

***

"I forgot to ask," Rachel said on the car ride back to Collinsville. "How'd all the interviews go?"

Cody sighed. "I think well. I've got a team put together. Good guys. They all have decent experience. It's just weird. The project manager is having me handle everything. All the paperwork. All of it. We don't have an HR person, so I don't have anyone to ensure that I am doing it all correctly. But, no one seems concerned. They may even plan to pay these guys under the table."

"What're you concerned about?" Rachel asked, not quite following.

"Well, I get the impression some of the guys might not be legal even though they have all of the needed paperwork," Cody said, concerned. "Who knows, I might be tapping into stereotypes. I think I just feel under qualified to be handling the entire hiring process."

"You are under qualified," Rachel said. "You're a carpenter, a specialist in period wood design, and an engineer; but you're not a HR person. That sounds sketchy, Cody. Why can't the people who hired you, handle the paperwork for the team you're hiring?"

119

"I don't know," he grumbled. "I'll talk to someone on Monday. I think my biggest problem with this job is being too accommodating. I don't know how to say no."

"Just say yes with stipulations, you know?" she replied. "For example, *I'm happy to interview and select the renovation team; but I am not comfortable with the legalities of the paperwork requirements. Or, I'd love to go to dinner with you guys, but I'll need to step out for a few minutes at 7 p.m. for a call with my kids.* When you let them know upfront, it might make them feel like you're going out of your way to spend time with them. You'd get the time you want with Sky and Slater, and make the time with your co-workers even more valuable in their eyes. It makes it clear you are working to accommodate them and doing something extra."

"Sheesh," he said with a laugh. "I don't know why this stuff is such a foreign concept to me. I mean, that sounds completely reasonable."

"You're just trying to do a good job. I get it. People in your position are typically just out of college or trade school and are supposed to be yes-men. You've been working for yourself for almost a decade. So, while this is your first experience with a job like this, you don't have to be a yes-man."

Cody smiled. "Again, it's so clear when you say it."

***

When they got back to the house, Rachel popped Slater into his wrap and raced to the kitchen to get dinner together for Skylark while Cody took her upstairs for a quick bath. As Rachel sliced grapes and cheese, she heard a phone chirp with a message. Remembering that they had both been phone-free all day, Rachel went to peek at her phone to make sure there wasn't anything important.

She noted a friendly message from Susan checking in, but nothing else worth responding to immediately. As she set the phone down, she instinctively placed it in the spot where she had put Cody's earlier. Thoughtlessly, she touched the home button to wake the screen and was shocked to see three missed calls and 11 text messages. Unable to see who they were from, she cringed to think they were all from his work or, even worse, Simone.

"What am I doing?" she asked Slater quietly. "I'm acting like I don't trust him."

She felt foolish for looking. Now, she was paranoid and worked up, while at the same time feeling guilty and sneaky. It had been such a lovely day and with one silly choice she felt like she had spoiled it. Massaging Slater's back through the wrap, she returned to preparing Sky's dinner.

Moments later Cody returned with a giggly, clean Skylark.

"Here she is, mom," he said, setting her in the highchair. "Shiny like a diamond and hungry like a hippo."

Rachel smiled, but it felt forced. "Like a hippo, huh?" she teased Skylark. "Well, dinner is served my dear."

After they got both kids to bed, they went down to make their own dinner.

"What do you think?" Cody asked. "I'm voting for something easy. Peanut butter and jelly?"

"Oh, we can do a little better than that," Rachel said with a laugh. "How about turkey sandwiches and a salad?"

"Sounds amazing. I'll take the salad if you do the sandwiches."

As Rachel gathered the fixings, Cody meandered over to the sideboard and picked up his phone. She watched with bated breath. His shoulders slumped forward and his brow furrowed as he reviewed the screen.

"What's wrong?" she asked.

"I have, like, 10 texts or so from work...and phone messages," he said.

"Oh no, is it anything important?"

"No," he replied, upset. "That's why it bothers me. You're right. This job's their social life. But, I can't get mad at that, right? They consider me a buddy."

The word *buddy* set her off, it made her think it was Simone reaching out to him. She was tempted to say he should be mad about it; but Rachel knew it was only her that was angry.

"Yeah, it's hard to be mad at people trying to make you their friend," she agreed, begrudgingly.

***

"Dr. Hamming's office," the receptionist answered.

"Hi, I was calling to confirm a business appointment I have scheduled with Dr. Hamming for today at 1 p.m.," Rachel replied as she double-checked Slater's car seat harness.

"Your name, please?"

"Rachel Brooks."

Rachel handed Skylark a doll to play with and inspected the diaper bag to make sure they had everything they needed for their trip to the city as she waited for the receptionist to return.

"Ms. Brooks?"

"Yes, I'm here," Rachel replied.

"You are confirmed for 1 p.m. with Dr. Hamming."

"Thank you." Rachel hung up her phone and took a seat behind the wheel.

"Okay, my little loves. Let's do this, shall we?" she said looking in her rearview mirror at both babies gazing happily into their own mirrors. "Off to the city we go."

***

Both kids were asleep when she double-parked in front of her dad's apartment building. She only had stopped once, at a fast food parking lot about half way, to feed Slater and give Skylark a chance to stretch. Both seemed to moan when Rachel strapped them back in for the rest of the trip.

Now, looking at the clock, she debated how long she could sit with them exactly before she had to wake them and take them upstairs. Five minutes, she concluded. That would give her just enough time to say hello to her dad and Pam, make sure the kids were squared away, and get to the meeting with a few minutes to spare.

Suddenly a delivery driver honked behind her. It sounded like the foghorn on a cruise liner. Both kids woke with a start and burst into tears.

Rachel rolled down her window. "I've got two formerly sleeping, now crying, babies that I need to take upstairs," she shouted, feeling her New Yorker roots reemerge. "Go around or wait!"

The driver waved and maneuvered his way around.

Rachel called her dad.

"Hi-ya, Rach," he answered.

"Can you come down and help me get the kids upstairs?"

"Sure, see you in a sec."

Rachel hurried to get both crying babies out of their car seats. Placing one on each hip, she did her best to comfort them and calm them down. When they saw grandpa approach, they both stopped and Skylark eagerly reached for him.

"Thanks," Rachel said, handing her to him. "They were woken up by a delivery guy honking, so they're both a little startled."

Joe laughed. "Yep, they're definitely country kids if car horns are waking them up. Horns are white noise to city kids."

"True," Rachel agreed, grabbing all of the kids' stuff with her free hand. "Cicadas, those are white noise for country kids."

She handed Joe a bag and they made their way upstairs.

"Oh, don't you look beautiful," Pam said greeting them all at the door. She took Slater and grabbed Rachel's hand to get a better look at her ensemble. "So professional. Dress suits, suit you...I want to make a better pun, but I'll spare you. It really is a good look on you."

Rachel laughed. "Well, thank you. It feels good to get out of the leggings and sweatshirts once in a blue moon."

She put Slater's milk in the fridge and gave both kids a kiss.

"Thank you so much for your help today," she said giving her dad and Pam a hug. "I should be back no later than 3 p.m., but it could be much earlier. This could be a quick meeting, I'm not sure. I'll text or call when I have a better sense of what to expect."

"Take all the time you need," Pam said. "We're pleased as punch to get time with these two angels. And, how fun for us to have them here!"

"Well, thank you. I'll see you soon."

Racing down the stairs, she was grateful to not see an officer anywhere in sight to ticket her illegally parked car. Getting behind the wheel, she texted Tom to let him know she was on the way. She put on some upbeat music and worked to move from mom-minded to lawyer- minded.

Arriving at Dr. Hamming's building in less time than she anticipated, she got a spot in the underground parking and took a moment to pray.

"Dear Heavenly Father, thank you so much for the opportunity to meet with Dr. Hamming. Please help him to be receptive to our proposal. Help us to get his trial re-opened and get Susan enrolled. Thank you. Amen."

She gathered her research and took a look at her face in the rearview.

"You've got this," she said. "You have to, for Susan."

***

Rachel's stomach flittered when she saw Tom waiting in the lobby. His coy smile as she approached made her feel flushed. The unexpected physical reaction flustered her. She wanted to reprimand her stomach and cheeks for their disloyalty, but felt a wave of guilt hit her at the same time. Tom's revised expression of concern made her wonder if he could tell she was a mess of emotions internally.

"You ready?" he asked.

"Yep, all set," she replied avoiding eye contact. She refused to get butterflies looking him in the eyes. It would just be too *wrong*.

"Everything okay?" he asked. "You look uncomfortable."

He still knew her.

"I'm fine," she managed, starting to walk toward the elevator a few steps ahead to avoid looking at his face. "Were you able to get any information on the participant who died?"

"Of course," he said following her into the elevator. "I spoke with his sister. His cancer was so advanced and immune system so low, he died from the flu. It had nothing to do with the trial. He had actually seen positive results from the trial as well."

"That's crazy," Rachel said. "Is there proof? Are there doctor's records or something that show it was the flu?"

"Yeah, the death certificate lists Influenza as the cause."

Rachel's ears popped as they reached the 21st floor. "This should be a piece of cake to get reopened then," she said, regretting the words as they left her mouth.

Tom gave her a look of admonishment. "It was going to be until you said that."

"I know," she agreed. "We're just superstitious, though. It should be fine, right?"

"We'll see, *D'Angelo*. We shall see."

Rachel bristled at the use of her maiden name. It seemed disrespectful. But, almost worse than the oversight, Rachel found comfort in the endearing way he said it. With no time to consider it either way, she brushed it off and opened the office door.

"Hi there, we have a 1 p.m. meeting with Dr. Hamming," she said to the receptionist.

"Your names, please?" she replied dryly.

"Rachel Brooks and Tom Pierson."

"Please have a seat. Dr. Hamming will be with you shortly."

They found two seats in front of a giant fish tank and sat down. Watching the tropical, brightly colored fish swim back and forth did nothing for Rachel's nerves. She was fired up. She knew deep down she had no right to be angry at Tom for anything more than an omission, but she couldn't help it. She was furious that she was still drawn to him and that her pure love for Cody was being tainted by her physical attraction to her former boyfriend. That was what it had to be, she thought, just something physical, chemical. She could take comfort in the fact that it wasn't emotional. Rachel was 100 percent dedicated to and in love with Cody…right?

"Ms. Brooks, Mr. Pierson; Dr. Hamming is ready for you."

Tom put his hand on top of Rachel's and gave it a reassuring squeeze. Had it been Cody she would have welcomed the gesture; but coming from Tom it just heightened her confusion. She quickly stood and followed the receptionist to Dr. Hamming's back office.

They entered into a small, but impressive space with corner windows and floor to ceiling bookshelves bursting with books. Dr. Hamming stood to greet them, surprising Rachel with his height. A handful of inches taller than Tom's 6-foot stature, she guessed he was 6'5". His curly, peppered hair was unkempt and in contrast to his bowtie and sweater vest peeking out from under an open lab coat.

"Thank you both for rescheduling. I seldom change or cancel appointments; it was just very unusual circumstances," he said, offering handshakes to them both.

"We understand," Rachel replied. "It was your aunt, correct? Is she okay?"

"She's still in the hospital. It was a stroke. She appears to be healing, though."

Rachel's heart lurched, remembering her own experience with discovering her Aunt Cali was in the hospital. Possibly projecting too much, she had to fend off tears thinking about what Dr. Hamming was going through. The irony was not lost on her either. Her experience was what broke the camel's back between her and Tom. When she received the call informing her of Aunt Cali's stroke, Tom had told her to wait and go in the morning.

"We've been through something similar," Tom said to Rachel's surprise. "Rachel lost her aunt a couple of years ago to a stroke…she was like a mother to her. Hope your aunt gets better soon."

Rachel looked at Tom, confounded.

"Thank you, both," the doctor said. "Now, let's chat. I hear you represent someone interested in helping re-open my cancer trial."

Rachel cleared her throat. "Yes, yes we do."

\*\*\*

Rachel had just finished laying out her favorite red and white checked picnic blanket when she spotted Cody strolling up the path holding take-out. Her heart did a flip-flop and she could barely control the butterflies, causing her to take note and give herself a little leeway for her stomach's behavior earlier with Tom.

Skylark caught sight of him too and pushed herself up to standing with Rachel's help, doing her best to totter toward him.

"There's my girls!" Cody shouted, starting to jog towards them.

He nearly dove onto the blanket embracing them both in a hug. He pulled Slater out of his carrier and held him as he leaned in for a kiss from Rachel.

"Aw, you guys, it's so amazing to have you here," he said, giving Rachel another kiss. "What an awesome way to end the day!"

Rachel smiled. "It is a pretty good day. I can't get over this weather. Why is it like 15 degrees cooler here than in Collinsville? Ocean breeze? Are you and the weather conspiring to get us here?"

Cody laughed. "Heck yes. I'm pulling out all the stops. The weather. Soon we'll have the New York Symphony Orchestra here to serenade the kids with lullabies, and then I'm working with the New York Lottery...our winning ticket is arriving any minute."

"Nice, I'll take it all," Rachel said. "But, honestly, it's been a pretty great day without it. The kids had a great time with my dad and Pam, the drive out here was relatively painless, and the meeting with the doctor went really well. He's going to support us in our efforts to lobby the FDA to get his trial re-opened. Now, getting to see you for dinner, it's awesome. If only I didn't have a two-hour drive home."

Cody gave her a crooked smile. "You know you don't *have* to. You're welcome to stay with me. I'm sure we could arrange to have two cribs brought up to the room."

Rachel pulled the food containers out of the bag and started to set it out.

"There's a chance it could be a very rough night," she replied after a moment of contemplation. "I mean it sounds good right now, but what if the kids don't sleep and we're both up all night?"

"We'd be up all night *together*," he said, almost giddy at her wavering. "I'm totally willing to take that risk."

She wanted to have the time with him. Having lost one of their days over the weekend and with how weird she'd been reacting to Tom, and with how needy Cody's co-workers had been, she desperately wanted to be together, as a family. She took a deep breath, hoping she was doing the right thing. "Okay, let's do it."

# CHAPTER SEVEN
## TROUBLE IN THE CITY

Rachel admired the view of the Hudson from the hotel window. It was a beautiful room, understated, clean, and modern. Crisp white linens contrasted against dark, sleek, wood furniture. The wall of windows reminded Rachel of her apartment with Tom. Rachel worked to push out the memory, as Tom was the last person she wanted on her mind. Skylark pushed her little hands against the glass and seemed awe struck by the height and grand city views.

"Sorry, I have to take this," Cody said apologetically, looking at his ringing phone.

Rachel nodded and he stepped into the hall. Looking at Skylark and Slater, she had a sudden sinking feeling. What was she going to do with two babies in a hotel room until bedtime? For the time being, Skylark seemed totally content waddling around and tossing stray papers, magazines and books on the ground. Slater was happy being bounced in the wrap, but Rachel wasn't sure any of it would last long.

The hotel room door opened and Rachel looked up expecting Cody.

"We should go out and look at the Empire State Building or something," she started.

Then she met eyes with a young bellhop pushing in the first crib.

"Sorry," she said. "I thought you were my husband."

He shrugged and smiled shyly. After pulling in the second crib from the hallway he stepped out quietly. Rachel examined the cribs and wondered how well they were cleaned. She wished she had sanitizing wipes. Cody's voice echoed from the hall and Rachel struggled to hear what he was saying as she bobbed up and down with Slater.

Finally he reentered the room and tossed his phone on the bed.

"How do the cribs look?" he asked.

"Fine," Rachel replied hesitantly. "Do you think we could go out for a little walk and stop by a Walgreens for some antibacterial wipes? I'm just wondering how many kiddos have gnawed on the bars since they were last given a good wipe down. Plus, I'd love to show the kids some of the city lights, too."

"Sure," Cody said. "Maybe we can pick up some toiletries and a new outfit for you, too? So you are comfortable tomorrow. It's my treat."

Rachel giggled. "Is that your gentle way of letting me know that you don't want to share your toothbrush?"

"No, it wasn't actually…but now that you mention it," he said tickling her. "Let me just change my shoes and I'll be ready to go."

Cody's phone buzzed on the bed with a text.

"So, is everything okay? At work?" Rachel asked trying not to pry.

"Oh, yeah, they're just all downstairs having a couple of drinks before dinner and wanted me to join. I told them I had a date."

Rachel locked Skylark into the stroller. "Why didn't you just tell them your family was in the city?"

"I don't know," Cody replied, gathering his keys and wallet. "I sort of feel like they're already too involved in my life. I'd kind of like to keep the most precious parts separate."

Rachel wasn't sure she totally understood, but the sentiment in Cody's delivery made her feel loved and valued, so she went with it.

As they headed out the door, Rachel noticed a woman approaching from the elevators. She recognized her, but couldn't recall from where. She wondered if she was a former client when suddenly Cody stiffened.

"Hey Simone," he said, a heaviness in his voice. "What's going on?"

Simone smiled casually, beautifully. Her sophisticated red lips outlined pearl white teeth. She was stunning.

"Oh, Cody!" she exclaimed, like a high school girl would excitedly tell a girlfriend a secret. "Is this your *family*?"

Cody looked annoyed.

"Hi, I'm Rachel. This is Slater, and Skylark is down there in the stroller," Rachel said, extending a hand.

Simone delicately took her hand, almost as though she didn't want to touch it, and then leaned forward and gave Rachel air kisses in the direction of each cheek.

"What a nice surprise to meet you all," she said, her French accent not quite as pronounced as Rachel had envisioned.

Rachel smiled, unsure of how to respond.

"*Well,*" Cody said. "We were just heading out."

"Sure, sure," Simone said. "I'll walk with you."

The lot of them made their way toward the elevator. Squeezing awkwardly into the elevator, Rachel finagled the stroller into the corner while Simone leaned nonchalantly against the handrail, one of her high-heeled feet positioned against the wall. She looked like a model posing for a perfume advertisement. Rachel wished she had on her power suit from earlier. Having changed when she picked up the kids at her dad's, she felt frumpy by comparison in her T-shirt, skinny jeans, and Slater in the baby wrap.

Finally the elevator dinged and they all stepped out. Cody held the door open for Rachel as she made her way out of the corner.

"You should come meet the team," Simone blurted out. "Come for one drink and see the dream team Cody's a key part of."

Rachel lifted a brow and gave Cody a look.

"I'd love to, but maybe another time when we don't have the kids in tow," Rachel replied.

"Yeah, we left their fake I.D.'s at home," Cody said, laughing at himself.

"Darn," Simone said, with a pouty lip. "The guys will be sad to have missed this."

Rachel took offense to the way Simone said *this* as opposed to *you*, or you guys, or all of you. The fact that she used *this*, made Rachel feel like she and the kids were a circus sideshow, something to be ogled and laughed at. She took a small inhale and reassured herself that Simone was not a native English speaker. It was most likely an honest mistake.

"All right, Simone, I'll see you tomorrow," Cody said, taking Rachel's arm and directing her toward the front door a bit forcefully.

As soon as they got outside, he loosened up. "Sorry, I just need us to get out of here. I couldn't stand the idea of her giving me those kisses one more time."

"She's intense," Rachel agreed, walking toward the Empire State Building. "But, the kisses aren't that bad — she just blows air really close to your face."

"I get different kisses," he said, causing Rachel's stomach to turn.

"Oh," she replied.

"So, we're walking all the way to Empire State Building?" he asked, a little concerned.

"No, just in the general direction. I'm hoping we're able to see the lights before we actually get to it. Maybe we'll take the kids to Times Square," she said.

"What do you think? It couldn't be any more intense than Simone, right?" she added with a laugh.

Cody rolled his eyes. "She's annoying and aggressive, but not big-city-mugger status."

Rachel bit her tongue to avoid saying anything snarky.

"Let's just look for a Walgreens," she said. Suddenly Slater started to cry. "Oh no, he's hungry."

Cody's eyes got wide. Rachel could tell he wasn't ready to head back to the hotel with the prospect of running into Simone or the team.

"Let's pop into this cafe," Rachel said, spotting a familiar chain. "You can get a drink and a cookie for Skylark and I'll feed Slater."

She could see his shoulders relax and she wondered why Simone had such a hold on him. Why did he let her get him so worked up? Then she thought of Tom and how she'd been reacting to him, because of how he made her feel...and her heart sank.

\*\*\*

Rachel awoke to a light knock on the door and hushed voices. Midway between sleep and consciousness, she

134

imagined it was Simone conspiring to steal Cody away. But, as she came-to, she was greeted with a coffee and a tray of room service with flowers.

"Good morning," Cody said with a sly smile. "How'd you sleep?"

Blinking, Rachel sat up and looked over at the kids who were both still sleeping happily in their hotel cribs.

"Really well, actually." She took a sip of coffee and smiled. "This is nice. Waking up with you, here. The city is so much more appealing in the morning than at night."

"What do you mean?" Cody asked.

"The energy seems to shift with the light. Do you feel it?" Rachel wondered, taking a bite of French toast.

"Wait until you get downstairs," Cody agreed. "The breakfast buffet is a totally different scene than the after-work bar scene."

"You mean we don't have to worry about your co-workers obligating you to morning coffee dates?"

"Oh, I didn't say that...," he paused and showed Rachel his phone.

"Three text messages? From whom?" Rachel asked, concerned.

"Simone," he replied, sounding defeated. "She wanted to know how you guys liked the hotel. If I wanted to walk to work with her. If I wanted my regular coffee. There's a very good chance she's on her way up right now."

Rachel tensed. "Really? Can you head her off in the hall? Before she wakes the kids?"

"Oh man, I was going to try and pretend like we weren't here," he said with an embarrassed smile. "But, I didn't think of that."

He started toward the door.

"Hey," Rachel said suddenly. "Do I need to be worried about anything? With her?"

Cody cringed and wagged his finger in the air in rebuke. Rachel relaxed and sunk back into the pillows, relishing the morning light and sipping her delicious coffee. However, the fact that he hadn't actually *said* there was nothing to worry about, bothered her. Within a minute, Cody was back in the room.

"Did she come up?" Rachel wondered.

"Nah, I just texted her back. I told her to not stop by because the kids were still sleeping. Not sure why I didn't just do that in the first place."

He dropped onto the bed next to her and took a bite of his breakfast sandwich.

"It's so great having you guys here," he said. "It's sort of counterintuitive, but it makes me excited to go to work."

Rachel raised an eyebrow, confused.

"Most of the time, I'm pretty down about everything when I wake up. I hate work for keeping me away from you guys until I actually get there. It always changes once I'm there, but the mornings before are pretty rough. It feels amazing to wake up on cloud nine and be able to head into work with a positive outlook…because I really do love the work I'm doing. I wouldn't put us through all of this if I didn't."

Rachel scooted closer to him and rested her head on his shoulder.

"I love you, Mr. Brooks."

A soft knock came at the door. Rachel turned to Cody wide-eyed.

"Is that *Simone*?" she mouthed.

Cody hopped up and rushed to the door. After looking through the peephole, he quietly cracked the door and stuck out his head.

Rachel could hear only the muffled hiss of a woman's whisper, but she was positive it was Simone. The collection of tiny red flags tucked away in her head were waving on high alert, like a color guard group in a marching band dedicated to making it known that Simone was trouble.

Cody pulled his head from the door and quietly shut it. He returned to bed with a new paper coffee cup.

"She'd already picked up a coffee for me," he said dryly. "Couldn't let it go to waste."

Rachel shifted, uncomfortable with the situation. Taking a deep breath, she looked at him and offered a sympathetic smile.

"I trust you, Cody," she started. "But, I don't trust Simone. She has no sense of boundaries and she's brazen. In my opinion, there's no way she'd be paying this much attention to you, if she thought of you as just a *buddy*."

Cody looked a little surprised.

"I've been thinking the same thing," he said. "But, I honestly think she's just lonely. She's been honest with me and she's just getting over a bad breakup, feels insecure in her role at work, and doesn't really have any friends. Since we have similar memories from Stanford, I think she's just sort of latched on. She doesn't have a good sense of people's personal space, but other than that she's harmless. Don't worry, Rach."

Rachel wanted to counter. She wanted to tell him to stop being so naïve, but she bit her tongue. He looked her in the eyes, as if to figure out what she was thinking. The connection made the butterflies in her belly go crazy. She leaned forward and gave him a kiss.

"I'm going to get ready before the kids get up."

***

"We're going to need money," Tom said.

Rachel took a sip of her coffee. She hoped Tom didn't notice the stall. Feeling in over her head as well as a little naïve for thinking they could simply take a handful of doctor's notes to Congress and get the drug trial re-opened. It was going to take a lot more than that. Trips to D.C. Wooing the lobbyists who had the right political connections. Even with Tom's pedigree and clout, they were going to essentially need to bribe people to hear them out and fast-track it through the right channels. And, it was all going to be done together, which Rachel vacillated between being incredibly grateful for and bitter about. What in the world was Cody going to think when she told him she had to go to Washington D.C. with Tom? It made Simone's shameless behavior seem innocuous.

"Let's make a list of all parties of interest," Rachel suggested. "I mean, Susan isn't the only woman out there with this form of cancer literally dying to get involved in an aggressive clinical trial. Since we have Dr. Hamming's word he'll include her, I say we push to garner as much additional interest as possible."

"I see your angle, but don't you think anyone who throws down a bunch of cash to have the trial reopened will expect to be included, too? We've got to be smart about this. It's not an open call. We need to get one pharmaceutical company behind it. Promise them an exclusive on the drug or something. Did Hamming say he was working with anyone already?"

"Yes, he'd been working with funding from Johnson and Johnson, but when the participant died they didn't want to be

138

associated. I believe he's no longer under any obligation to them, but we'll need to confirm."

Tom looked at the coffeehouse's tin ceiling like it was going to provide answers. As he tapped a pen to his pursed lips, Rachel got a good look at his sculpted jawline. She always liked that feature. Burying her head in her hands she tried to think about something else. But feeling ashamed of the attraction and forcing herself to suppress it, only made it worse. It seemed the more she tried to find Tom repulsive and annoying, the more she was discovering all of the qualities that attracted her to him in the first place. Suddenly her breath felt sharp and shallow and she felt a rush of anxiety, thinking the third cup of coffee for the day was a bad idea.

Building upon the feeling her mind began to snowball with everything happening in her life. The more she tried to get things done for Susan, the more hoops she had to jump through. The more she tried to trust Cody, the more brazen Simone became and the more nonchalant Cody acted. And then, Slater and Sky; was she neglecting them by taking on too much?

Rachel felt the walls of the quaint country cafe closing in on her. The claustrophobia that enveloped her was unlike anything she'd ever experienced.

"I'm going to grab some water," she mumbled, and tried to make her way to the bar.

Somewhere between her seat and the coffee bar she felt her legs become noodles and had to will herself to move forward. Sweat droplets dotted her upper lip and forehead and she wondered if she wasn't coming down with food poisoning.

"May I have an ice water?" she asked the barista.

"It's 10 cents for the cup," he replied not picking up on her urgency.

Staring at him, unable to express her need further, she dropped onto the closest bar stool and rested her head on her arm. Taking a slow, shallow breath, she prayed for help. Every thought that entered her mind seemed to aggravate the tension and cause her to feel more and more desperate for air. It had been such a welcomed offer when Tom volunteered to meet her in West Point, saving her another drive into the city. Just over an hour from Collinsville it was an easy morning trip, as opposed to a full-day trip into Manhattan. But now, with the way she was feeling, she felt trapped. At least if she was in the city she could have called Cody or her dad to come and get her. Here, her only option was…Tom.

"Hey, Rach?" he said from behind, seemingly summoned by her realization. Placing a comforting hand on the back of her arm he slid an ice water close to her hand. "What else can I get for you?"

"Can we go outside?" she asked, taking a sip of the water. "I feel like I can't breath."

Tom helped her off the barstool and gently guided her out to a table under the shade of a large oak tree. After getting her seated, he walked back inside to get their things. The green leaves on the ancient branches above her flittered in the soft summer breeze, capturing Rachel's attention momentarily and helping her to calm slightly. After another sip of water, she closed her eyes and was able to feel a gentle gust of wind blow past reminding her that Tom was not her only option, Holy Spirit was there, too.

"Dear Heavenly Father," she said silently. "Thank you. Please help me to calm down at least enough to get home safely and figure out what in the world is going on."

She took a deep breath and opened her eyes. Tom was sitting across from her. He smiled, concerned. "It's a lot to get done, huh?" he asked, knowingly.

Rachel nodded. "Yeah, I'm feeling better though. I just needed some fresh air."

"I know we can do this," he said softly. "I want to do this for you, for Susan, for everyone else who needs this trial re-opened. But, I'm not going to do it if it is going to hurt you, overwhelm you. Of course you want to do what you can for Susan, but your first priority is to yourself and your family. If this is spreading you too thin, there are other ways to help her without killing yourself."

Rachel shook her head. "Thanks, Tom. Really, I appreciate it. I'm not sure what just happened. There's a lot going on, beyond this. I think it was just the culmination. I'm fine."

She took another sip of her water and Tom stared at her.

"You sure?" he asked. "I'm not positive, but I think you just had a panic attack."

"No, no way," she said. "I'm fine, honestly. I think I may just be coming down with something. I should head out soon."

He continued to search her face, unconvinced.

She hated that he still knew her so well.

"Okay, then, next steps," she said, trying to rally all of her energy. "I'm going to confirm with Dr. Hamming that he's no longer tied to any specific pharmaceutical company. Once we get the information, we can start to go after the other big ones for money and lobbyist connections. I'll really want your help in our approach. You've got that natural salesman thing."

Tom looked distracted. "Sure," he said.

"Great," she said, starting to gather her things. "I think we're good for now, right?"

"Rachel," he replied. "If you think I'm going to let you drive home after I just watched you nearly hit the floor, you're mistaken. I'm either driving you home in your car or my car."

Her immediate reaction was to revolt and refuse adamantly. Who was he to be so self-righteous? However, as she tuned into her limbs, she realized her hands and legs were still vibrating with nerves. Determined, she pushed herself to standing only to wobble like a newborn calf. She looked at Tom, defeated.

"You have time to drive all the way out to Collinsville?" she asked.

"No, of course not," he said with a smirk. "But, those are your options."

She exhaled as she debated what to do.

"Let's take your car," she replied. "Cody can pick up our car on his way home on Thursday night."

"Does he take the train?" Tom asked.

"Yes."

"You know what?" he started. "You caught me on a giving day. Let's just take your car. I'll take the train back to West Point to get my car. My day's already shot."

He was right. Rachel knew it. She was going to feel like she owed him, big time, which was annoying; but she appreciated his willingness. Actually, she questioned it, but was having a tough time thinking of another option.

"Okay," she agreed. "Thank you. When we get to town, you have to let me get you lunch though."

"Deal."

***

Maybe *Cali's* wasn't the best idea, Rachel realized. She could feel familiar eyes staring at her from every direction as she and Tom entered together. To compensate she added additional space between them.

"Hey, Rach!" Maddie exclaimed. "Where's the fam?"

"Susan's got the kids and Cody's still in the city, this is Tom, an old friend from the city," she said unsure of how to properly introduce him. "He's working with me on trying to get Susan into a cancer trial."

"Pleasure to meet you, Tom," Maddie said, extending a hand. "Are you guys here for lunch? What can I get for you?"

"Something healthy, big, and filling," Rachel said. "I had a rough morning. I feel like I need some nutrients and I'm sure Tom's starving."

"You got it. Any drinks? Iced coffee?" Maddie asked.

"No!" Rachel said with a little too much emphasis recalling her anxiety from earlier. "I mean, not for me. Tom?"

"Sure, I'll take one for my trip home," he replied. "So, Maddie, I've got an hour. What do I have to see before I leave?"

Maddie looked suddenly sheepish. "Well, Collinsville is famous for Cheesecake Yogurt. After you eat lunch you should definitely get one of those, or at least taste it. Then, we have a beautiful park…," she started.

"Ah, I've got a pretty good park, too," he replied cutting her off.

Maddie nodded and went to get their food.

Rachel took comfort in seeing the dismissive characteristic of Tom she didn't like. It was refreshing in some odd way.

***

"How was your day?" Cody asked through the phone.

"Fine," Rachel said slowly. "Tom had to drive me home."

"What? Did the car break down?"

"No, I got sick, actually," she said quietly. "It was incredibly compassionate of him. It blew his whole afternoon."

"Are you okay? I don't get it? What happened?" Cody's face contorted with concern. Rachel wished she couldn't see him through the screen. It made her want a hug, which wasn't possible and it made her miss him more.

"Don't worry," she said. "I'm fine now. I did some self-diagnosing online and I think it was a little anxiety attack. I'd had too much caffeine and was feeling a lot of pressure with everything we have to do for Susan and the feeling just took over. It was pretty scary how debilitating it was. I thought I had food poisoning."

"An anxiety attack, like a panic attack?" Cody asked, his face only becoming more and more grave. "Should I come home? Is it too much being by yourself with the kids every day?"

"Cody," Rachel said seriously. "I'm fine. Really, I'm all better now. I think it had a lot to do with the caffeine. This whole thing, trying to get the trial reopened is going to take a lot more work than I anticipated. It may even require a trip or two to D.C. We're going to need to seek funding from a major pharmaceutical company. It's just a lot and I just got sort of panicked with the idea of it all. But, I've got a game plan together now and feel much better about the whole thing."

"Well, I'll come home if you think it would make you feel better," he said.

"When you put it that way. Yes, please come home," she said.

Rachel laughed sadly to herself. "No, I'm fine. I'm excited to see you Thursday night. Enough about me. How was your day?"

"I was hoping you'd forget to ask," he said.

"Why, what happened?"

"ICE officers, you know, immigration, stopped by the work site today," Cody said. "They took one of my guys."

"What does that mean?"

"I'm not sure, but it's not good," he said, disheartened. "The thing that really bums me out is this was something I was worried about. It's the reason I didn't want to have anything to do with the hiring of these guys."

"When will you have more information?" she asked.

"I have no idea."

"Wow," she replied, stumped. She was struggling to find the benefits of this job, but didn't want to push the point with Cody any further. "Well, I hope tomorrow's better, for both of us."

"How're the kids?" he asked.

"Good. They were with Susan this morning, who is doing incredibly well. I admire her so much. She always has a smile. It's really tough to tell how she's feeling, but it sounds like her doctor is great. This afternoon, we just went and spent some time in the park."

"Give them hugs and kisses for me?" he said. "This job just continues to make me wonder if we made the right decision, you know? I really miss you guys. Any thoughts on coming back out for another night soon?"

"Last week worked out well," she said. "I just need to buckle down and focus on getting this trial reopened, though. I can't lose valuable time sitting in a car or a hotel room, unless I need to be out there...which it sounds like there will be plenty of opportunities ahead. So, to answer your question: yes, but when I have to head to the city for work."

"Fair enough," Cody said with a sigh. "I love you, Rach."

"I love you too, Mr. Brooks."

Rachel turned off her phone and looked around the kitchen. Reviewing the day, hearing the news about Cody's trouble with immigration, brought feelings bubbling up in her chest reminiscent of her fit earlier. She could feel the anxiety surfacing and her concern of having another attack at home alone, while responsible for two babies, was making it worse. She quickly stood and turned the T.V. on to a mindless, funny home makeover show. Taking a deep breath, she exhaled slowly. With the comforting chatter in the background, she got on her knees and prayed.

"Lord, I feel so lost. I'm uncomfortable with life right now. My own skin feels unfamiliar. My marriage with Cody is such a blessing, but living apart doesn't feel right. I don't think moving the kids to the city is the best solution; but am I looking at it wrong? Is it best that we be together as a family no matter what the circumstance? I don't know? Besides that, I'm so embarrassed about my attraction to Tom, especially when I've been so condemning about Simone. And, then, I'm afraid there's actually something to worry about with Simone. I'm worried about Cody's job. I'm worried about Susan. I need her to get well. I'm terrified I won't be able to get this trial re-opened for her, for a number of reasons; not the least of which is my fear of continuing to work closely with Tom. It doesn't feel right. To top it all off, I *really* want to be a great mom. I want to be present for Sky and Slater. I want to be kind, patient, loving, and long-suffering, just as you have been with me. I am finding it really hard when I am focused on so many other things. I love you. I'm sorry for treating you like my therapist, but I am lost. I feel like I'm spinning out of control and don't know how to stop. Please be with me, Lord. Please bless me with Holy Spirit's presence and help me regain my footing and find…me. In your name I pray, Amen."

Rachel opened her eyes and wiped at the tears wetting her cheeks. Pushing herself off the ground and taking a seat on the couch, she felt better. She had faith help was on the way. She didn't know how or when, but she knew it would come.

"Thank you," she whispered softly.

# CHAPTER EIGHT
## BLINDED BY THE LIGHTS

The view from the hospital room was not nearly as grand as the one from her hotel room. Disillusioned with the nondescript skyscraper just feet away, Rachel closed the blinds to the glaring sun and underwhelming view and returned to her seat by Susan's bedside.

She lay quietly, propped up by pillows, with her eyes closed. It bothered Rachel how angelic Susan looked. She was beautiful in her wig, even with tubes sprouting from her arms. Rachel was not ready to view her friend in any sort of heavenly context. If Rachel had any say, Susan was keeping her feet on Earth for the time being.

"It's so hot outside," Rachel said, softly. "I can feel the heat radiating through the window."

Susan opened her eyes and smiled. It wasn't the beaming Cheshire grin Rachel was accustomed to, but it was a reassuring smile nonetheless.

"I'm glad they have good air conditioning here," she replied. "It makes it easy to snuggle in and read a book or doze off while I'm getting treatments."

"How're you feeling?" Rachel asked.

"Fine," she replied with a sideways smile. "Under the circumstances, remarkably well."

Rachel stood and laid a consoling hand on Susan's leg.

"You look amazing under the circumstances. It's like you're the Princess and the Pea, you're so perfectly poised and coiffed, surrounded by all these pillows. You're making me feel a little disheveled over here."

They both laughed.

"The wig's pretty good, right?" Susan said, touching the blonde ringlets.

"It's stunning," Rachel agreed. "I'd never know it wasn't your real hair, if I didn't know your real hair so well."

Susan nodded and smiled.

"Pastor Bishop likes it too," Susan said with a wink. "To be honest, I'm not sure he realizes it's a wig. Which is fine by me. The less he realizes I'm sick, the more normal my life is and the less sick I feel…"

She seemed lost in thought for a moment and then added, "Men, you gotta love em! He's never had an eye for detail, but has big appreciation for aesthetic."

They both laughed, until Susan stopped with a grimace, apparently feeling a pain from the pressure on the IV in her arm. Rachel took a breath and tried to hide the emotion that hit her seeing her friend in pain.

"Thank you, girl," Susan continued.

"For what?" Rachel replied, incredulous. "I haven't done anything yet."

"Oh, girl. Thank you for being *here*. Thank you for all of the work you're doing. I'm so grateful for everything. Who knows, this trial may be doing more harm than good. I sometimes feel like it is. I wasn't losing any hair until I started here. Rachel, I know it's a huge undertaking to get Dr. Hamming's trial re-opened, but please know it's not in vain. I believe it's my best shot at getting healthy. I've known since the beginning that you'd be the one to help me through this and you've exceeded my expectations every step of the way. You're amazing."

Rachel met Susan's eyes and shrugged.

"I love you, Susan. You've been there for me more than half my life. I'll always be there for you."

***

"Okay, you win," Rachel said, offering Cody a big smile.

He looked into the phone confused.

"What'd I win?" he asked.

"I was teasing, but what I'm really trying to say is that I'm willing to give moving the family to the city a try," Rachel said, happily. "The reasons are just stacking up, making me think it's the right thing to do."

"Really?" he said, excitedly. "What brought about the change of heart?"

"Well, it's been weighing on me since we realized it could work. But, now, with all of the meetings to get the trial re-opened and Susan getting treatment in the city, it just makes sense."

His face dropped a bit. Rachel noted his disappointment, but was distracted by Skylark who was done with her breakfast and tossing the leftovers to the floor.

"Skylark's so excited she's tossing her eggs in celebration," Rachel said, taking the phone over to her highchair. "Say hi to Daddy."

"Hi, sweet girl," Cody said. "So, Rach, when were you thinking? When do you plan to move out?"

"Well, as soon as possible. I don't see it as permanent by any means. It's just for the time being. So, I envision us staying with you at the hotel and still spending weekends back in Collinsville. What do you think?"

"Why the rush now?" he asked, not quite as enthusiastic as Rachel had imagined.

"There are so many pressing things happening," she replied. "Susan's in the city three days a week and I'd like to be there for her as much as possible. I have a handful of meetings in the next two weeks with big pharmaceutical companies. And, of course, the sooner you, me and the kids are all back together as a family, the better, right?"

"I'm glad I'm at least in your top three reasons," he said with a smirk.

Rachel's cheeks flushed. "Cody," she pleaded. "C'mon, you know what I mean. Our family's always been reason one to even consider it. I'm still hesitant. I'm still nervous about having the kids in the city. But, nearly every other aspect of my life is dragging me back to the city. It just seems unavoidable at this point. The perk of it all is that we get to be together."

"I know," he said. "I'm beyond happy, well, relieved actually, to have you all out here regardless of the catalyst. So, are you thinking we'll all head out together Sunday afternoon?"

"Yeah, unfortunately the Sunday summer potlucks are going to have to end early this year. I'm sure people are going to be bummed; but hopefully we'll be able to start them up again next year with *all* of us there."

"Yeah," he said quietly.

Rachel shrugged. "That wasn't meant to be a morbid thought or a premonition that we'll still be dealing with the same back and forth that we are now. I just really want to take this time to work hard and figure things out for all of us. I pray that by next summer the Bishops, you, our family, all of us, can be together again, healthy and happy."

Skylark started fussing almost instantly followed by Slater. Rachel carried the phone back over to them.

"Hey, you two," she said tickling Sky. "What's going on over here? Can you talk to Daddy a little bit more?"

Skylark adamantly shook her head no and Slater's cries began to escalate.

"Looks like we're done talking for now," Rachel said, laying the phone on the counter and picking up both babies. "We're going to head into the living room so Sky can play and I can feed Slater. We love you. See you tonight?"

"Yep, I should be home by 10 p.m."

*** 

The HOV lane was moving at a clip compared to the other traffic entering the city. Congestion on a Sunday evening, you had to love densely populated metropolitan areas, Rachel thought. Turning around, she discovered both kids were sound asleep which didn't bode well for their bedtime in a few hours.

Cody, already a pro at the commute, seemed happy as a clam speeding past the solo drivers, his family in tow. Rachel on the other hand was feeling a bit anxious with the decision. It felt as if they were taking a major step back in some way.

Rachel felt as though she was surrendering to the city. She envisioned stepping into her mom's shoes and it was terrifying. She worried that living in a hotel room was going to drive her and Cody to some semblance of what her parents' relationship was like. It worried her to even consider they could ever end up in a similar situation. She took a deep breath and stared out the window at the fast approaching skyline.

"Almost home, guys!" Cody announced, causing Skylark to flinch and wake crying.

Rachel turned around and worked to calm her before she woke Slater. She grabbed Sky's pacifier and popped it in her mouth.

"Were they sleeping?" Cody asked sheepishly.

"Yeah," Rachel said softly. "It's okay, though. They needed to wake up or they'll never sleep tonight."

Rachel stroked Sky's head as she stared at the big buildings out the car window.

"Should we drop the bags off at the hotel and then go to a park for a bit?" she asked. "I'd like Sky to be able to run around before we try and sit down to dinner somewhere."

"Sure, we could even get a hotdog at the park. Have a little picnic dinner?"

"That might be good," Rachel sighed. "I'm going to need to get my head around not having a kitchen. I can't eat out for every meal. We'll need to get a hot plate for the hotel room. It won't be ideal; but I'll at least be able to scramble eggs or make pasta in a pinch."

"Sure," Cody said again. "Whatever'll make you and the kids more comfortable."

Rachel found it strange to be co-parenting with Cody again. His weekend visits had been such a whirlwind, trying to fit in as much love and fun time as possible, it hadn't been real life. As Rachel reflected, she realized they had gotten into some bad habits by celebrating his every Thursday night return. She doted on him, while he became the kids' plaything, and in turn their roles had become unbalanced. She was just as guilty, if not more so, than him for the upset, but the realization put her on edge.

She noticed a lack of attention from him lately on details that he would have previously noticed. Being too loud when the kids were sleeping, forgetful of nap and meal times, noticeably disengaged when they started to get fussy; it was understandable, but a little unsettling. Cody had always been the *good* parent. He was the one on top of everything, helping Rachel to get her act together. He was still an amazing dad, but he had set his own bar pretty high and was dipping a little below the baseline lately.

*Ask how he's doing,* a quiet voice directed from her heart.

Suddenly embarrassed, Rachel realized she hadn't asked him about himself in a number of days. She had been so focused on getting things together for the city, informing people of the move, getting ready to meet with the pharmaceutical companies, and taking care of the kids, she had been totally caught up in her own things. And, here she was condemning him when she had absolutely no idea what was happening in his life.

She cleared her throat as they pulled into the parking garage. *It's not a good time,* she thought. We've just arrived at the hotel, the kids are awake, we're going to need to get out in a minute, *I'll ask him later.*

*Ask how he's doing,* emerged again.

"Cody?" she asked.

He looked at her and smiled as he searched for a parking spot. "Yes?"

"I realize I've been distracted by the move and have been pretty self-absorbed. How are things? I don't even know what happened with the immigration stuff at work."

He looked at her again with a solemn face.

"You've got a lot of stuff going on," he said softly. "Things are fine. The immigration stuff's not good, but the company's getting it figured out. The mistake is going to cost them a lot of money. And, while no one's directly pointing fingers at me, I get the impression they are behind my back.

It's put me in a weird position with everyone and deep down makes me feel like my job could be on the line. Simone's actually come to my rescue a few times, making it clear that hiring wasn't part of my job description and that it's upper management's mistake for passing if off on me."

Rachel's stomach turned. She had blocked out the thought of Simone. While she was grateful someone was coming to Cody's defense, it irritated her that it was the woman who she already felt so threatened by.

"I don't even know what to say," Rachel said truthfully. "I'm sorry you've had to deal with all of this and I didn't even realize."

Cody pulled into a parking spot and patted her leg.

"Honestly it's been so upsetting, I'm glad I didn't have to rehash it at the end of the day. There was a moment or two when I thought I was going to lose the job for sure and all of this stress I put the family under would have been for nothing. It seems to have worked itself out now. I'm just concerned about what'll happen to Jaime though."

"Who?" Rachel asked.

"My employee," Cody explained. "The guy immigration picked up. I hired him a little unsure about his status, but he seemed like the perfect guy; and he was. He's just a little younger than me, has a wife and two kids, is a crazy hard worker and incredibly talented at woodwork. Anyhow, it was a mistake. He's being sent back to El Salvador where he has no family and actually had some trouble with gangs. I don't know what it means for his family or for him."

Skylark and Slater were fussy and ready to get out of the car. Rachel looked at Cody.

"We should pray for him and his family," she said.

"That'd be good," he agreed. "Tonight during family prayers, I don't think these kiddos can handle another second."

Cody got out and unloaded their luggage and grabbed Slater. Rachel got Skylark and the stroller and they made their way upstairs. As they emerged in the busy lobby, Rachel was struck by the number of people and the club-like atmosphere. She found it abrasive and worried that it might be over-stimulating for the kids. Turning to Cody, she was just about to request they hurry to the other elevator when Simone appeared with a wine glass in hand.

"Hello!" she exclaimed. "The family's back."

Cody's shoulders stayed square and he offered her a pleasant smile.

"Yeah, everyone's here to stay for a bit," he replied cheerily. "Rachel's got some work in the city."

"Well if you need any tips on where to go or what to do, let me know," Simone said, addressing Rachel.

"Thanks," Rachel replied. "I actually grew up here. I chose to leave after college."

"Ah, well then, as you know, the best places change in the flash of an eye," she said provocatively.

Simone leaned forward and gave Rachel two air kisses, seemingly even further away from her face than before.

"A few of us from work are getting a drink, Cody. If you have time to join, it would be a great opportunity to get some face time with Alex," she said, pointing to the bar.

Cody looked conflicted.

"Let us get our stuff upstairs and I'll see if I can come for a bit," he said.

Rachel was surprised he was actually considering it and she was disappointed to see his guard was no longer up with

Simone. Her coming to his rescue over the illegal hire had most likely put her in his good graces. It annoyed Rachel.

"Well, if I don't see you...," Simone said, leaning forward and giving Cody a kiss on each cheek.

Rachel could feel her cheeks flush pink with anger. She hated the fact that Simone could so easily irk her, but even more, she despised the fact that she had the gall to go after Cody so openly. She bit her tongue to keep from saying anything she might regret.

Walking down the hall to their room, Rachel took in deep breaths and worked to control her emotions. She could tell Cody wanted to say something.

"Did you want to go down for a drink?" she asked him.

"It's not really a matter of whether or not I want to," he replied. "I really do need to get some face time with Alex. Along with Gary he's the money and power behind this renovation project; and the one who's getting all of this immigration stuff settled."

"Oh," Rachel said working to hide her disappointment.

She thought for a moment. The timing was really bad. The kids needed to get out and have dinner soon or they would lose their minds.

"Why don't you go and spend some time with them, relax," she said. "It's not like you can really win him over if you have to leave in 20 minutes. Go, be part of the group. I can take the kids, get dinner and play a bit."

He looked surprised.

"It's definitely not ideal," she added. "But, I get it. And, I can't make the kids wait while you chat with them. These things always take longer than expected."

He nodded. "I'm sorry, Rach. I probably should've anticipated this."

"It's totally not a big deal," she said. "There'll be plenty of other opportunities to get out as a family."

"Are you going to be okay on your own?" he asked, concerned.

"I'll be fine."

***

The overflow of Times Square tourists spilled out onto 9th Avenue. Rachel had chosen the route in hopes of avoiding excessive foot traffic, but the crowds seemed to entertain the kids so she tried to go with the flow. She had forgotten how energizing the city could be. Hot summer nights in particular made the city come alive. Everyone spilled onto the streets to get out after dark when the sun-beat asphalt and concrete had cooled and the lights came on.

So many lights and things to look at, even blocks from Times Square the action never ceased. Rachel found herself reminiscing of her life in the city before the kids and Cody, before Collinsville stole her heart and she lost Auntie Cali. She wondered if things would have been different. Laughing at herself, she reminded herself of the life she was living and her relationship with Tom.

"Yes," she replied quietly to herself. "Things would've been *very* different."

But, would things have been better, she wondered. There was so much extra money and time back then. Even with her high stress job as an attorney, she recalled getting out, meeting friends, going to dinners, watching concerts in the park, going to yoga. She thought about the rut she and Tom had fallen into, the superficiality of it all and the daily monotony.

Looking down at Slater and Sky, their little eyes wide with intrigue and surprise as they took in everything happening around them, she had a wave of gratitude hit her.

158

Sure, things may have been easier in some ways, but living the life of a New York attorney and being married to Tom would have always felt superficial and monotonous. Her life today was filled with more love and joy than she ever thought possible. She was truly blessed and felt bad for even entertaining herself with the idea of *what if.* Life with Cody and the kids in Collinsville was incredible and maybe this momentary setback, being back in the city, was supposed to remind her how good she had it.

Observing the crowds, street vendors, shops and restaurants, Rachel took note of the seemingly never-ending variety. With so many choices, people were bound to make some good ones and bad ones. Rachel was so grateful that she had been given the chance to turn her series of bad choices around and make a good one by leaving Tom, moving to Collinsville, getting back involved in church, and finding the love of her life. It seemed like life had become illuminated when she chose to leave the city and her life there. She wondered if it was the change of scenery or her own internal transformation that had made those changes possible.

Maybe her life with Tom could have been just as satisfying had they both taken some time to develop and refine themselves as individuals. Tom had changed since she was with him. There was a certain level of awareness and thoughtfulness that hadn't been present before. And, he was now dabbling with religion, which was shocking. Had she seen Tom the atheist reading the Bible back when they were together, she would have passed out thinking she had just witnessed a miracle. But, whether it was her leaving or his own personal growth, he had emerged a better person and she prayed he continued down the path to a relationship with God.

As they approached Central Park, Rachel got excited remembering when she used to go with her mom. She was eager to share it with Sky and Slater, even if they were too little to really appreciate it.

Just like when she used to go, there were food carts, balloon vendors, horse drawn carriages, and street performers. Only in the summer was it this full of life. Of course the city was always teaming with people, but steamy days sent locals and tourists alike to the streets at night to revel in all the city had to offer. The park was not the same on a Monday night in October. This was special.

Both kids were taken with a flamenco guitarist performing at the entrance to the park. Rachel pulled Slater from the stroller and swayed with him while Skylark clapped her hands together enthralled with the music. They all danced for a while and then spotting a favorite hot dog vendor, Rachel bee-lined the stroller through the other revelers and placed an order.

After getting two dogs with the works, she took the kids to a nearby bench and took a seat. She handed Sky half of a hot dog and watched her closely as she picked at the bun and nibbled at the meat.

"It's good, right?" she asked her daughter.

Skylark nodded in agreement and focused on the bun.

"It's too hard for you to eat like this, huh?" Rachel took the plastic knife out of the bag and cut the meat into little pieces. "My mom and I used to come here and share hotdogs, too. I'm sorry you don't get to meet her. You would've loved her. And, oh, she would have loved you. If she was still alive, we'd probably have to live in the city. She never would have allowed my babies to be more than five minutes from her."

Skylark was happily eating and not paying much attention to anything Rachel was saying. Slater realizing it was dinnertime, began to fuss and so Rachel quickly finished her dinner. Getting him situated under the nursing apron, Rachel continued to reminisce about her childhood in the city. She began to wonder if raising the kids in the city was really so bad.

In the distance she could hear another live performance starting, but this sounded like a stage play. The city was in good form, giving Cheesecake Yogurt and Collinsville Park a run for their money.

***

"So what'd you guys do?" Cody whispered, so he didn't wake the kids.

Rachel tried hard to not be annoyed by the late return and light scent of alcohol on his breath.

"We just went to Central Park and wandered around," she said softly. "I think the kids really enjoyed it."

"Isn't the park dangerous?" he asked.

"Well, it's just like the rest of the city…you don't want to wander around alone late at night where no one else is around. It's like a party when the sun first goes down this time of year. We got hotdogs and watched a play. How was your face time with Alex?"

Cody cleared his throat.

"Ah, he left right after I got down there," he said. "I got to speak with him for a minute. He seemed happy to see me, but his daughter had a piano recital he had to get to."

Rachel debated what to say. Inside, her brain was screaming, *And, why didn't you call to let us know? Why didn't you come join your family?*

But, her heart knew it wasn't the compassionate thing to do; she bit her tongue.

"So, what'd you end up doing?" she asked, struggling to sound curious and not prying.

"Well, I got the latest information from the rest of the team. They filled me in on the latest with the immigration stuff. Then, we had dinner and discussed the week ahead. I would've much rather been with you guys. But, it was like you said, once I was down there it was hard to break away."

"What's the latest on the immigration stuff?"

"The development had to pay a fine of $25,000," he said making a disgusted face. "But, it's apparently because the company has been hit for hiring an undocumented worker previously. The attention and blame is off of me, thank goodness, and has been turned to hiring practices. They're looking into bringing on an HR person."

"That's great news!" Rachel exclaimed as loudly as she could without waking the kids. "Did you guys celebrate?"

"Nah," Cody said with a laugh. "I think I'm the only one that's been really worked up about it. No one else really cared, they just filled me in."

"Oh, I thought you guys maybe had a round of drinks or something," she said shyly. "I've never really seen you drink, but your breath smells like alcohol."

"I don't drink, really," he said, looking a little defensive. "Simone bought a nice bottle of wine at dinner and insisted I try it. Rather than make a big deal of it, I took a glass. But, I tried to make it last all dinner. I didn't want her to pour me more."

Rachel should have guessed it was peer pressure from Simone. It was petty and ridiculous to make someone feel like they needed to drink. It was just another incident for Rachel to add to her list of reasons not to like her. She got up from the couch where she had been preparing for her meeting with Merck. The drug company was eager to make headway in oncology pharmaceuticals and had expressed great interest in Dr. Hamming's study.

She wasn't sure what else to say to Cody. It was disappointing to her that he was in this situation. She didn't think it was his fault, but she wasn't impressed with the way he was handling the various curveballs. It was like the job, the people, the circumstances had totally wounded his ability to make decisions and be confident in himself. She didn't want to admit it, but it was hurting her opinion of him as well. She knew she needed to be supportive. After all, he had helped her through, and with all the awful sides of her personality he had witnessed without judgement, it was her turn to take care of him, listen, and not analyze or criticize.

Embarrassed for her train of thought, she went to the bathroom to get ready for bed. When she returned Cody was smiling broadly.

"You're so beautiful," he said.

"Aw," she replied with surprise. "What made you realize that right now?"

"I don't get to tell you enough," he said. "I often think it at moments when it would be completely off topic or distracting to tell you. I love you, Rach. I'm so grateful to have you guys out here. You are my love, my wife, my best friend...you're my life. It's been terrible being away from you. After everything we've been through in the past year and a half, it just seemed really wrong to be apart. I haven't felt like myself. I know this isn't ideal, but it feels right."

She got into bed next to him and rested her head on his chest.

"I love you," she said. "We're a great team. We do better when we're together."

Listening to his heartbeat was always soothing. The two of them together were a great team. She realized, resting there, that her wandering mind and criticism of Cody was purely an emotional defense mechanism. Maybe deep down she was afraid that she would end up like her mom one day. Regardless, the separation had put her fears and insecurities into overdrive, causing her mind to work overtime protecting her in the worst way possible — an overactive imagination, anxiety, and vulnerability.

It still didn't make it good, or right, or respectable, but that's what her visions of Tom and spite for Simone stemmed from. As long as she didn't indulge in it and reminded herself of the love she felt for Cody, *this* connection, everything would be fine.

"I'm glad we're here too," she said. "The kids love it. I think in my mind I had demonized the city a bit. I'd built it up to be this place that represented the negative aspects of my childhood. But, being out tonight brought back so many wonderful memories of my mom. I just realized that in many cases it was the city that brought me escape and solace from what actually were the negative aspects of my childhood."

Cody kissed the top of her head.

"That's a pretty major realization," he said.

"I know," she said dreamily. "I'd always attributed those feelings of safety, joy, and freedom from pain to Collinsville; because it was such a defined escape from the hard times at home. I mean, I physically went from the city to the country, leaving all my worries behind. But, the city was my friend every other day of the year. If things were hard at home, I could get out and be surrounded by people, distractions, activity, and fun."

She considered what she had just said.

"Anyhow, that's just my longwinded way of saying that I'm excited to share the city with the kids and I'm sorry for being so resistant before. I love you so much, Cody. I think being separated has impeded my judgment in some ways."

She lifted her head to look him in the eyes. He kissed her forehead and her nose.

"I'm still on the fence," he said. "The city has a lot to offer, but it's not Collinsville. It's not home."

To Rachel's dismay, he started to get up.

"I've got to get ready for bed," he said. "I have to be into work early. We're having a walk-through with Alex and some of his counterparts to review the first floor. Oh, and then, I've got to do dinner with the team tomorrow. This time it's an actual work thing. The management is taking us all out to see a new property they just purchased. Who knows if there's wood, but I'm being lumped into the group for the excursion."

"Really?" Rachel asked, failing to hide her disappointment. "Where is the new property?"

"Chelsea," he replied.

That was close to where Rachel lived when she was with Tom. She suddenly wondered if he still had the same apartment they had owned together. She would like to see it again. Catching herself, she returned her thoughts to the conversation at hand.

"Okay," she said quietly. "Maybe we'll go visit Susan and my dad tomorrow. I'll figure something out. So, do you think you'll be able to do dinner with us sometime this week?"

"Sure, yeah, of course," he replied, sounding like he was trying a little too hard to be convincing. "I'll check with

Simone. She'll know what's okay to ditch and what I should be at."

Rachel watched him walk to the bathroom, hurt the conversation had changed so drastically. Unsettled, she stood and followed him; stopping at the bathroom door, she leaned against the frame as he brushed his teeth.

"Do you trust her?" Rachel asked honestly. "Do you think Simone's got good intentions?"

He spit and turned to face her.

"I hadn't really thought about it," he said, earnestly. "I've known her for a long time. She's always been a little…I don't know…passionate, but she's never seemed malicious or untrustworthy. She's done a lot for me recently. She's the reason I have this job."

Rachel realized he didn't see what she did. She wished she hadn't brought it up and began to retreat to the bed.

"Don't worry, Rach. She's harmless."

Rachel wasn't so sure. She crawled into bed convinced she wasn't going to sleep a wink. When Cody returned she pretended to be asleep. She listened as he turned out the light and checked his phone. When she heard his breath deepen, she climbed out of bed and started busy work, tweaking the Merck presentation and trying to calm her own building anxiety and suspicion.

# CHAPTER NINE
## THE DINNER INVITATION

It was shocking to Rachel how quickly her dear friend had deteriorated. It had been less than a month since she was watching Sky and Slater while Rachel went to meetings in the city. Today, Susan's skin looked ashen and her spirit seemed bruised.

Grateful that Pam offered to take the kids to a water playground for a few hours, Rachel sat at Susan's bedside holding her hand while she was given another concoction of drugs intravenously. She wasn't chatty, so Rachel sat there in silence going between silent prayer and daydreams. She tried to not replay last night's conversation with Cody in her mind, but focusing solely on words of prayer for Susan's recovery was proving mentally and emotionally exhausting. So, of course, her brain selected another emotionally volatile topic to dwell on.

She didn't understand why the conversation went from such a sweet, loving space to something so distant. Recalling the feeling she had laying on Cody's chest, was calming, but his inability, or unwillingness, to see Simone's menace was irritating. Especially after Rachel had finally voiced her concerns outright, she found his dismissal a little bit disrespectful.

Suddenly her phone vibrated with a text. It was a baseball emoji from Tom. A relic from their relationship, the icon meant he thought the final presentation she had sent him to review was a home run. His digital pat on the back made Rachel smile and eager for their big meeting.

Another text immediately followed: *My uncle wants to join. Are you available for a run-through tonight or tomorrow AM?*

Rachel almost jumped out of her seat.

"Susan?" she said softly. "I just got some wonderful news. District Attorney Pierson is going to help us."

Susan perked up and looked at Rachel. Her eyes twinkled from behind heavy lids and dark circles.

"*The* District Attorney Pierson?" she asked.

"Yes," Rachel said excited. "You remember, he's Tom's uncle. Tom must've said something to him. I'm guessing he thinks getting a successful cancer trial re-opened will look good on his resume. But, regardless of his reasoning, this is so good for us."

"Let's pray, girl," Susan said, patting Rachel's arm.

Rachel bowed her head and squeezed Susan's hand tightly.

"Dear Lord, we are beyond grateful for your goodness," Susan started. "We love and adore you and just want to come to you in thanks. Thank you for guiding Rachel to this trial, for opening the doctor's heart to our plea, and bringing on Tom and D.A. Pierson to help. Thank you for bringing Rachel to the city to be with me in my time of need. This experience has been such a blessed reminder of your presence and your role in our lives, Lord. Thank you. In your name we praise you, Amen."

"Amen," Rachel repeated.

She had tears in her eyes, overcome with emotion. Susan's prayer had opened her eyes to all of the strength, support and goodness surrounding her. She was in awe of Susan's spirit and faith, offering sincere gratitude in the midst of battling cancer. And, whether Matt was interested in participating for superficial reasons or the goodness of his heart (Rachel suspected the two worked in tandem), she was overwhelmed with his willingness to lend his name and title in support of their efforts. And, Tom, well, he was continuing to impress her. While she was grateful for it, it wasn't making any of this any easier. She didn't want to feel any more endeared to him than she already did. Especially while feeling ousted by Cody.

A nurse waltzed in and began to remove needles and tubes.

"Mr. Bishop's here for you," the nurse said in a sort of singsong.

"Pastor Bishop," Rachel corrected. "He's the pastor of Collinsville Community Church."

"Ah, I see," she said with a nod. "Well, Susan, Pastor Bishop's here. Right on time as usual. He looks tired."

"He hasn't been sleeping well," Susan agreed. "I don't think any of us have. We're going to need a Hawaiian holiday when this is all over."

The nurse laughed. "Now that's something to look forward to; a vision to help you through the hard days!" she exclaimed.

"Yes, ma'am," Susan said.

The nurse helped Susan in a wheelchair and began to push her to the door.

"Linda?" she asked. "Can I have a couple of minutes to get myself together?"

"Sure, doll," she replied. "I'll see you Friday. I'm heading out for the afternoon."

Linda the nurse made her way out and Susan looked at Rachel.

"Hey, girl, I know I look like death. I can't have John see me like this. The wheelchair's already going to freak him out. Can you please fix me up?"

"Of course," Rachel replied taking Susan's makeup bag.

She gingerly began applying foundation and blush, and carefully styled Susan's wig. With a touch of lipstick and mascara, she looked close to her vivacious self. Close. Rachel pushed her to the mirror and let her evaluate the job.

"Wow, Rach, you've got some hidden talents," Susan said, clapping her hands together. "Thank you, sweetie. Really. Thank you for being here with me. I've forbidden John. I just don't want him to see me with all the tubes and needles."

Susan shuddered and smiled.

"But, I really don't want to be here alone," she added. "It's scary...and depressing."

"I'm so glad that things have worked out so that I can be with you," Rachel said. "It really is a reminder that God is watching over us."

Overcome by Holy Spirit's presence, Rachel tried to stifle the tears pushing to make their way out.

"I've been so resentful and bitter about Cody taking the job in the city," she continued, wiping at a stray tear. "But, it's ended up being a true blessing in disguise. Only He knows what we need. And, I needed to be reminded of that."

"Me too, girl. Me too."

***

Looking at the response from Cody for the fourth time, she tried to detach emotionally and understand the situation from his perspective. She had texted him as she left the hospital about watching the kids while she went to prepare with Tom and D.A Pierson in the morning. She knew he couldn't do it tonight, because of the big work excursion; but she had hoped he'd be willing to take a bit of time off in the morning.

She was already relying on Pam to watch the kids for her formal meeting with Merck later in the afternoon and after having her watch them today, it felt like too much of an imposition to ask for the morning, too.

Cody had typed back that he couldn't, *I have to be at work.*

Sitting in her dad's living room, taking a moment to catch up with Pam and Joe before taking the kids, she debated what to do. Her dad was telling a funny story about Sky pulling herself up at the water playground using another toddler's bathing suit, but Rachel was struggling to pay attention.

"But, much to the chagrin of his mother, the little guy seemed perfectly happy going commando," Joe said with a hearty laugh.

"Oh my, that's hilarious," Rachel said. "So, Pam, you're really okay taking the kids again tomorrow at 1? My meeting's at 2. I should be back by 5 at the very latest. It could be much earlier."

"Of course," Pam replied. "It's such a pleasure to get to see these little angels more. And, while we love Collinsville, I'm feeling pretty spoiled having them delivered to our doorstep."

"Okay," Rachel said hesitantly. "Well, I'm going to restrain myself from asking too often. I want you to continue to enjoy your time with them!"

Getting their things together, Rachel made a decision to text Tom the truth.

*Sorry for the delay. Was trying to rope in a sitter, to no avail. I could do tonight or tomorrow morning; but I'd have the kids. It'd be a distraction and not terribly professional.*

She watched as the dots appeared indicating his response. Then they stopped. Feeling unqualified and a bit second-rate, a full-time mom playing make-believe lawyer, she tucked her phone away and prepared herself for a snarky remark.

"Thank you, both, so much," Rachel said, putting Sky and Slater into the stroller. "I'm so grateful for your help. One of these nights when Cody's not working late, we'll have to go out to dinner. Our treat."

"Totally not necessary, but we'd enjoy that," Joe said, leaning down and giving Skylark a kiss on the forehead.

He lifted Slater's little hand and gave it a gentle fist bump. "Is Cody picking you guys up?"

"No, no," Rachel said. "We're going to walk back to the hotel. Cody's working late tonight, again."

Joe opened his mouth like he wanted to say something and thought better of it.

"It's pretty far, princess," he said. "Like 25 blocks."

"Uptown to downtown blocks are a breeze," she replied knowingly. "It'll be less than half an hour. I could use the walk."

He rubbed her back and gave her a hug. "Once a city girl, always a city girl."

Pam came over and gave her a hug too. "See you all tomorrow."

As she waited for the elevator, she heard her phone ding with a new text.

*Dinner at my parent's at 5. Eat, then mom will watch kids while we prepare.*

Continually surprised, her mind reiterated. Tom was proving to be everything she had wished for when they were together. Of course there were always glimpses of his best self back then, but they were elusive and fairly infrequent. Now, it seemed his natural state.

Feeling awkward and a little disloyal to accept the offer, she considered what her other options were. There weren't any, and no thanks to Cody, she thought. Plus, if she was being honest with herself, while there would be some uncomfortable initial greetings, Rachel really liked the Piersons. She liked Tom's mom, his dad, his uncle, their dog, and she really liked Tom. It would be a nice, if not necessary, way to spend the evening. Especially when comparing it to a depressing hotel room some 30 stories above a swanky, club-like bar and restaurant.

*See you at 5.* She typed, and not giving herself a moment to reconsider, she clicked send.

Looking at the time, she figured they didn't have the luxury to head back to the hotel first. They would need to make their way through Central Park to the Upper East Side now, to make it by 5 p.m. Taking a quick scan, she evaluated herself and the kids. They looked cute, but not old-money, Upper East Side-cute. All history aside, she still wanted to make a good impression and show the kids at their best.

Fishing through the diaper bag, she found her make-up bag and some new outfits for the kids. Her outfit was extremely casual, but would do for a hot summer night if she added a little oomph to her face. Starting down West 68th Street, she took in her surroundings. After Queens, she was surprised her dad had ended up in such a comparatively homogenous section of the city. All of the buildings were bleak and boxy and there wasn't much by way of shops and restaurants nearby. Well, he had to walk a couple of blocks. There wasn't anything directly downstairs, which for most parts of the world wasn't a big deal, but in the city it was an oddity.

As they approached the park, Rachel's heart started to race. At first she feared a wave of anxiety, but when she stopped and paid attention, she realized it was pure excitement. She was looking forward to her walk through the park. She was delighted at the idea of spending time with Tom and his family. She was eager to prepare for the big meeting tomorrow. And, she was excited that Sky and Slater got to join her for all of it.

Her phone rang.

"Hey," she answered. "How's work?"

Cody exhaled.

"Good," he said. "We're just getting ready to head out on our *excursion*."

"Why do you sound upset?"

"I think I'm just tired," he said. "How're you? The kids?"

"We're great," she said. "They had an awesome day with Pam and I got some great news…"

"Oh, that's so good," he said interrupting. "I'm sorry, Rach, I want to hear all about it; but they're rounding us up."

"Okay," she said. "We're going to…"

"I love you," he said. "See you tonight."

Rachel looked at her phone, astonished. She never dreamed she could feel even further away from Cody actually being in the same city. Taking a deep breath, she shook it off. There was too much to be grateful for. Coming from a place of feeling extremely isolated and emotionally alone to a place

174

where she now had an extended community of friends and family nearby and offering support, she couldn't let Cody's distraction with work bother her. Just today she had spent a quiet afternoon with Susan, enjoyed downtime with Pam and her dad, and was in the process of walking to have dinner with people she considered old friends.

In Collinsville, she had the church, Maddie, and her staff at *Cali's*, but none of them had time or were close enough to her situation to realize she needed love and encouragement. Many of them weren't even fully aware how often and how many days a week Cody was in the city. And, while Rachel could have reached out more, she hadn't for a number of reasons. Regardless, she was grateful to be in a place where she had so much support, even if it wasn't coming from the place she had expected.

On their walk to the Pierson's, Rachel took the kids by the lake where they stopped for a few minutes to watch the rowboats coasting across the glassy water. It reminded Rachel of the pedal boats on the lake in Collinsville's park and she felt homesick for a fleeting moment. Skylark was mesmerized. Rachel took the opportunity to sit on a bench, apply a little make up, and feed and dress Slater. When they were all set, she changed Sky while trying to explain why they could no longer watch the boats; she was still resistant to leaving.

In light of her excitement, Rachel was a bit surprised by the turn of events. Had someone told her a few months ago that Tom would be impressing her and she would be spending time with his family, she wouldn't have believed it. With a shrug, they exited the park and made their way into the beautiful old money neighborhoods of the Upper East Side. She easily navigated the path to the Pierson's stately, classic brownstone flagged with perfect potted foliage that evolved with each season. Come the holidays, the large planters would be filled with small Christmas trees with tiny twinkle lights. She always loved the holidays at their home.

She looked at the stairs leading up to their front doors and sighed. Not about to risk Sky and Slater's wellbeing, she texted Tom for assistance.

He emerged within seconds and Rachel found herself brushing aside the fact that she found him handsome and chivalrous. He was a friend, she told herself. Someone she had history with who was being supportive in the way a friend should be.

He offered her a quick, reserved side-hug and grabbed the front of the stroller to help get it up the steps.

"Thank you for being so accommodating," she said, unstrapping Slater and pulling him into her arms.

"It's nothing," he replied. "My mom couldn't wait to get her hands on your kiddos."

Rachel knelt down to unstrap Sky.

"You're going to carry them both?" he asked surprised. "At once?"

She laughed. "Consider it my workout for the day."

"Hand me the little dude," he said reaching out his hands. "Carter? Sutter? No, Slater, right?"

"Uh-huh," Rachel replied, astounded.

She gently handed him Slater and watched with surprise as Tom took him into his arms with relative comfort and confidence. Turning back to Sky, she pulled her out.

"Sky, do you remember Tom? You met him last year when you were brand new," Rachel said.

Skylark gave a shy smile and buried her face in Rachel's shoulder. Tom cracked an uncharacteristically sincere smile and laughed.

"My mom's going to be in heaven."

Rachel hid her smile behind Skylark's head and took a deep breath as she prepared to enter the once familiar home under completely new circumstances.

As Tom ushered her in and shut the door behind them, Rachel heard Mrs. Pierson's matronly voice carry through the walls.

"Rachel?" she exclaimed, from the dining room.

"Hi Stella," Rachel replied hesitantly.

Within seconds, she peered from around the corner and whisked down the hall to greet her. Estella Pierson, who went by Stella, was the pinnacle of old money New York, while at the same time the most mom-mom she had ever met. Even amidst all of her philanthropic work with The Met, The New York City Ballet, and more, she still found ample time to always ensure fresh baked cookies and homemade lemonade. If Rachel was being honest with herself, Stella was who she had in mind when she pictured the perfect mom. It was who she aspired to be.

"Oh, dear me!" Stella clasped her hands together at her chest when she saw Tom holding Slater. "I can't even! It's too much. Tom, give me that sweet child."

After taking Slater into her arms and covering him with red lipstick kisses, she waltzed over to Rachel and embraced her in a big hug, before almost inhaling Sky (who giggled at every kiss). Rachel found herself beaming, so much so that her cheeks hurt.

"This is such a wonderful surprise," Stella said, linking elbows with Rachel and guiding her into the dining room.

"We're all so excited to have you, Skylark, and Slater. Even Ed was pleasantly surprised by the news, and he's never pleasant about surprises. And, if you think I'm joking...well, you know."

Stella let the thought trail off and set Slater down in the sweetest infant bouncing seat. It appeared brand new. Rachel envisioned her calling the local baby boutique and having it delivered.

"Charlotte is coming in with the salads in just a minute," she said taking Sky from Rachel's arms. "Make yourself comfortable, I'll go round up the troops...I think everyone's in the yard with cigars or scotch, or both."

Sky didn't even look back as she was stolen away, she was smitten with Stella. Rachel was chopped liver. She looked at the beautifully dressed table and took a seat by Slater and next to the perfect highchair that was placed on the perfect spill mat. She felt like she was in movie and couldn't believe this lifestyle was once upon a time normal. Caught up in the moment, she was startled when Tom sat down next to her and snapped his napkin open to place it in his lap.

"Told you she was going to be in heaven," he said. "I'll be surprised if we get any of them to the table. They're all baby crazy. It's like I dashed their hopes and now they're all crazy for the pitter-patter of little footsteps."

Rachel felt her cheeks warm. She was solely responsible for ruining their expectation of grandchildren sooner, rather than later. She had made the right decision in her life by leaving Tom, but this was a painful reminder there was collateral damage.

"Are you ready to have kids?" she found herself asking him.

Tom took it in stride. "No, there's a few things that need to fall into place first."

Rachel nodded. "Are you dating anyone?"

He looked surprised. "Dating, yes. Anyone special, no."

"Sorry, I didn't mean to pry," she said. "I guess I was just wondering how close they might be to actually getting a grand baby."

"Not close," he said starting to fidget with his fork.

Suddenly everyone spilled into the room at the same moment Charlotte and her assistant brought out the salads, while Tom's younger sister, Lisa, District Attorney Pierson and his wife, Louise, ambled to their seats. Mr. Pierson circled over to greet Rachel.

"Welcome, stranger," he said.

Rachel stood to say hello and was greeted with an unexpected hug.

"Thank you for having me and the kids," she replied.

"Well, good luck getting them back," he said heading to his seat with a laugh.

Rachel hadn't anticipated the warm welcome. She knew they would be well behaved and polite, because it was just who they were; but she never thought they would be actually happy to see her. Settling back into her seat, she started to reminisce on when this was her family. Dinners were always an occasion, seemingly something special and formal. She loved that there was a salad fork, a first course, a table flagged by patriarchs of the family who engaged with everyone and enjoyed the company even more than the food.

As she placed her napkin in her lap and responded to various inquiries about life in Collinsville, she felt at home. It was a startling acknowledgement. Even more so, the presence of the feeling had her aware that she hadn't experienced it in a long time. She turned to Skylark who was happily eating, being entertained in a sublimely coordinated effort by Stella, Lisa, Charlotte and Louise. As one would stop to talk to the group, laugh at an anecdote, or take a bite of food, another would lean-in keeping her utterly content. Even Slater seemed at ease beyond measure, being lulled to sleep by steady bounce of his chair and friendly conversation.

Rachel couldn't think of a time when she was able to enjoy an adult dinner with the kids present. It was always someone scurrying off with one of them to go keep them busy elsewhere. This was nice.

The salad plates were soon replaced by the main course of perfectly grilled chicken, fragrant rice, and a tropical mango salsa. Tom splashed a little wine into Rachel's empty glass and she debated whether or not to drink it. While it seemed appropriate, she didn't want to have to pump and dump or risk being second rate for the meeting tomorrow.

As she chatted with Lisa and Louise, and watched Skylark happily wolf down the chicken and rice, and even the salsa, she wondered if her issues with Tom were really worth having given up on all of this. Had she stayed with him, she would not only have been financially set, she would have had a large, tight knit group to call upon for support.

But, as she lifted her knife to cut into her dinner, she remembered what was missing. There was no family prayer, no thanking God for all that He had provided, no blessing of the beautiful food, or offering up gratitude for a beautiful evening together as a family. They didn't know Him, and while the home was filled with love, it wasn't filled with His Spirit.

Suddenly the food no longer tasted as amazing and the conversation lost a bit of its luster. When they had all finished,

Rachel ducked out for a moment to feed Slater in the library. Stella followed and asked if it would be okay to take the kids upstairs to play, read stories and have a bath while she met with Tom and Matt.

"Of course," Rachel replied, surprised. "I have their pajamas in the diaper bag. I will grab them when I'm done here."

"Oh, no need," Stella said. "Louise and I did a little shopping this afternoon. Please just indulge us. Her son's grown and away at school. And, while my kids are around... they're not very cuddly anymore."

Rachel giggled and handed Slater to her.

"He's all yours," she said. "Stella, thank you for everything. I haven't been able to be this hands-off, ever. I've had a wonderful time tonight."

Stella smiled, waiving her hand as if to dismiss the thought, and danced away with Slater. Rachel pulled herself together and grabbed her notes for the meeting. She found Matt and Tom still at the dining table lingering over espresso and debating whether Scotland or Hawaii had better golf courses.

"You ready?" Tom asked, standing.

"All set," she said.

***

"Your research is solid," Matt said, commending Rachel on the information and statistics she'd found. "I think with the narrative and patient files Tom acquired from the deceased participant's family, and my commitment of support, this meeting will be a success."

Rachel felt her heart rate increase with gratitude and excitement. She was so energized by the work they were doing. Even if it wasn't to literally save the life of her dear friend, she knew it would still be meaningful work to her.

Gathering her notes, Rachel realized she had a missed call and text from Cody. He was home from his dinner. She sent a text asking if he could pick them up and finished gathering her things.

"How are you getting home?" Tom asked.

Her phone dinged.

Taking a look at the message, she replied, "Cody's on his way. He says about 15 minutes."

"Okay, should we go out and wait for him?"

Rachel found it to be a little bit odd. It was like she was Cinderella about to go from princess to pumpkin. She felt so welcomed throughout the night and was suddenly being ushered out.

He directed her to the front hall where Stella was pushing the stroller back and forth in perfect rhythm with two sleeping, angelic babies inside. She quickly put a finger to her lips to motion for silence and then leaned in to give Rachel a hug good-bye. She could see the other party members through French doors having a nightcap in the library. With a quick wave she said good-bye and Tom helped her out with the kids.

Out on the sidewalk Rachel continued to push the stroller like a piston, quietly watching the cars pass by. It was almost 9 p.m. and the summer sun had just officially set. Still warm out, Rachel thought a nice walk would be the ideal way to end the night and was disappointed that she would soon be squeezing into a car with two potentially crying babies. Back to reality, she thought.

"Can we talk for a minute?" Tom said softly.

All at once Rachel felt on alert, her nerves on edge. Knowing him well enough that he wasn't about to discuss arrival time for the meeting, she braced herself for an admittance of some sort.

"Okay," she replied.

"I'm enjoying working with you on this," he started. "I think we're going to do a lot of good, for a lot of people, not just Susan. But, I think it would be best for me if we limited our time together. After we get the pharmaceutical brand on board, I would like to request that you allow me and Matt to handle things, taking it to DC, and moving forward with getting the FDA's approval."

Rachel felt like she had been punched in the stomach. After all of the work they had done together, proving that they were a great team, why wouldn't he want her on board? After he'd been so kind and impressed her in so many ways, why would he hang her out to dry when she was feeling butterflies?

"I don't understand," she said. "Did I do something wrong? I thought we worked together so well…it felt like the old days, but even better."

"Exactly," he said. "Working with you has reopened a lot of confusing feelings, and painful emotions, that I thought were gone. Rachel, I loved you. When we're together, I'm reminded that I still love you. I find myself getting excited to see you and then reality hits and I feel heartbroken all over again. It's just too hard."

Rachel knew how difficult it was for him to admit his feelings. In his vulnerability, she could feel his honesty and pain. She envisioned hugging him and giving him a passionate kiss to heal his heart and fill her own desire to feel needed and loved.

"I don't want to hurt you," she said slowly. "I totally understand. I've had some mixed emotions, too. How could we not? We're a good team."

A car pulled to the curb and Rachel turned to wave at Cody.

"Thank you, Tom," she said, brushing her hand at his arm in a weak attempt to comfort him. "I'll see you tomorrow at 1:45 p.m."

He waved to Cody and put his hands back in his pockets as he walked the steps to the front door.

"You know my mom's going to want to see those kids again," he added.

Rachel smiled. "Anytime."

Cody met her at the curb and without direction gently pulled Skylark from the stroller and took her to the car. Rachel carefully pulled Slater from the stroller and transferred him to the car seat holding her breath in the hopes of not waking him. By the time she was done, Cody already had the stroller and diaper bag put away in the trunk. He greeted her at the passenger side and embraced her in a hug.

"Sorry I was so short earlier," he said. "The executives showed up earlier than expected and immediately started a sort of meeting on the move. It was hard to break away."

Rachel could tell their conversation, or lack of, had been on his mind all night too, which made her feel better. She was happy to know it wasn't their norm.

"It's okay," she said, trying to be nonchalant. "I tried to tell you we were on our way over here."

"I know you did. Was it to prepare for your meeting tomorrow?"

He opened her car door and helped her into the seat.

"Yes," she said. "Since I had the kids, the Piersons sort of made an evening of it."

"Did you have a nice time?" he asked starting the car.

"I did," she paused, feeling overwhelmed and emotionally drained. "…I had a very nice night."

"Glad to hear it," Cody said with a sigh. "Mine was…not very nice."

Cody sounded as exhausted as she felt. She knew a couple of follow-up questions expressing concern would be the right thing to do, but she just didn't have it in her. She gave his leg a gentle pat and closed her eyes. The significance of Tom's confession just moments before weighed on her. She felt like she had lost an old friend. Their new relationship had been such a welcomed link to the aspects of her past; the parts she had forgotten, but loved about her old life.

# CHAPTER TEN
## GO TEAM

The group collectively celebrated in a subdued tone — handshakes all around. After the Merck people left, as Rachel was packing up her computer, she felt a dark cloud come over her. It should have been the opposite. She should have felt lighter, triumphant, relief. The meeting was a success. Merck was in, backing the trial and financially backing their efforts in the Capitol. But, the only thing she felt was disappointment that her role was now basically done.

Matt walked over and threw his arm over her shoulders. "Great job, D'Angelo. Truly, you are a force to be reckoned with."

She smiled and picked up her bag, looking in Tom's direction wondering if he was going to say anything about the win, the incorrect use of her maiden name, *anything*.

"So, when will you guys head to DC?" she asked Matt.

"We're on the next train out of here," Tom said curtly. "Monday's Labor Day. People are going to start checking out Thursday. We have some meetings lined up for tomorrow in the hopes we can push something through when Congress is back in session on the 4th."

Rachel was confounded. "Is that how it works?" she asked surprised. "You can make it move that quickly?"

"We know some good people," Matt said with a wink. "Plus, with Merck, myself, and the results of the trial prior to being shut down, it's sort of a no-brainer. I'm confident the FDA will see it our way."

"That's wonderful news!" she replied, debating whether to call Susan right away or keep it mum until she heard something concrete. "I'm so grateful to have you two doing this. If it's not too much to ask, will you keep me in the loop? Text me anything exciting, good or bad?"

"Sure, sure. Tommy will let you know," he said already half way out the door for another meeting. His entourage was waiting for him in the hall, ready to walk and talk on their way down to the car.

Alone in the room with Tom, she wasn't sure what to say. She wanted to hug him, thank him, celebrate with him, anything really. She just didn't want to pretend they weren't friends, or that she didn't care about him and everything he had done for her.

"This is coming together so quickly, just like I've been praying for," Rachel said quietly.

He looked up from packing his papers and nodded in agreement. "It's another reason I like working with you. It's like there's a silent person on the team, helping to drive things through. Completing day-to-day projects as a lawyer can be like trying to ram through a brick wall…even the stuff that should be simple. But, with you, we tackle the impossible and it feels easy."

"You're right," she replied realizing the truth of his words. "It doesn't make sense that things would progress so fast. God has given us supernatural favor and we're on His timeline now."

Tom had once again pointed out the obvious. Rachel was always saying how blessed she was, but she rarely stopped midway to see God's hand in the actual process of things. She tended to pray and figure if she was fighting for what was right, God would be on her side to help her through. Throughout Skylark's adoption process and now with the cancer trial, it appeared to be true.

"It's awesome you're able to see it," Rachel said. "It's hard for me a lot of the time, in the midst of a trial, to actually see God's hand in it."

"Well, it's easy in this case," he started. "I mean we're a good team and all, but…"

Rachel knew where he was going. "Yeah, we're good, but we're not *that* good."

"Exactly," Tom said quietly. "Matt and I will be in DC tonight. We've got a number of meetings lined up tomorrow. We should have some answers on things by the end of the day. I'll keep you posted. Sprinkle some pixie dust, do a rain dance, or maybe say a prayer for us, the extra help is appreciated."

"Of course," she replied, looking him in the eyes. "You're in my prayers always."

She could read a mix of emotions on his face and wondered if she had overstepped a boundary.

"Thank you again for doing this, Tom," she added.

"It's my pleasure."

*** 

The meeting had gone so well and so quickly, Rachel was done for the day way sooner than she ever expected. Pam and her dad had the kids back at the water playground for the afternoon, so there was no need to rush back.

An afternoon all to herself, she mused a bit befuddled. After a moment of trepidation, she thought about the conversation with Tom and came to her senses. She knew exactly what she wanted to do. Slipping on her flats, she bee-lined for Central Park. It felt as though she couldn't get there quickly enough, but knew a woman in a power suit sprinting could cause alarm.

As she approached the black iron gate, her heart beat with excitement and the world around her stopped as she raced toward it. Upon entering the park, it seemed as if everything disappeared. The tourists, the runners, the meanderers, the hockers, everyone drifted into the background and Rachel slowed her pace. She found a quiet bench under a tree and took a seat.

"Dear Lord," she started hesitantly, feeling like it had been a long time since she had spoken with him, sincerely. Standing up, she knew she needed to prayer walk, spend time with Him and spend time listening. "I'm so sorry I haven't been around much lately. I keep getting so caught up in the day-to-day of everything and relying on my own my agenda to carry me through. It's not working. Heavenly Father, I need you. I'm so unsure of things lately. I'm questioning everything. My marriage to Cody, my ability to be a good mom, my move to the city…it all seems unsteady. I'm even questioning myself and my own judgment. For example, I'm wondering if Tom hadn't have been so decent, if I wouldn't have done something regrettable down the line. That's not me! That's not who I am. I love Cody. I'm so grateful to have him. I just feel so alone right now. I don't know where he is, he's so distracted with work. Susan's sick…and getting worse. My dad and Pam are great, but I can't talk to them about this sort of thing. I just feel so isolated. I feel *lost*, Lord. Completely and utterly lost."

As Rachel reached the depths of her soul, she began to get frustrated. She found herself crying. It wasn't what she was expecting. On her way over, she had envisioned her time with Holy Spirit in the park much less emotional, more pleasant. Wiping at her eyes with the back of her hand, she self-consciously looked around. No one was paying any attention. Another great thing about a city as big as Manhattan was that it was so easy to go unnoticed.

She took a deep breath and tried to calm down. As she worked to re-center her focus and listen to Him, she found herself by a beautiful weeping willow swaying in the late afternoon's summer breeze. Holy Spirit had always comforted her through the touch of a gust of wind, a soft wisp of air. She took a seat on the soft grass and watched the long branches swing back and forth.

She had spent so much time lately thinking about what her life would have been like had she stayed with Tom. Finding herself more than once wondering how her life would be different if she had the wealth and clout that came with being a Pierson. It just proved how lost she had become. It wasn't in line with who she was or who she was striving to be. The Lord knew that, but she hadn't gone to Him for direction.

She realized, left to her own device, she was taking the easy road. What came naturally to error-prone humans, wasn't the path to righteousness. It's so simple to focus on and consider the *what-ifs* in life, she thought. It's much harder to appreciate and see clearly what actually is.

Looking at all she had, Rachel was provided with an overwhelming sense of awe. She loved her life. She loved Cody so much it took her breath away. When she considered the idea of losing him, especially at the hand of her own weakness and failing, it made her feel sick. The love she had for Skylark and Slater had brought her closer to God than anything else she had ever experienced. Their home and life in Collinsville was more than anyone could hope for. She had her dream and then some. Looking back on her self-importance made it clear just how short-sighted she had been lately.

Humbled, she turned skyward. "Father, thank you. Thank you for so perfectly reminding me of all that I have. Please forgive me for neglecting to see everything right in front of me. I'm so grateful. I know we'll get through this challenging time. I just feel so far from you. I long to feel Holy Spirit with me, helping me through this. I thought by doing your work, your will, I would feel you presence. I came here to support Cody, to keep our family together. I came here because I love Susan and I want to help, but I'm feeling sidelined and confused. Even though I am so grateful for Your patience and love, I would love to feel You here with me. Where are You?"

Rachel rested her head on her knees feeling emotionally drained. She watched the willow's swinging branches sway with the breeze. Suddenly a gust of air enveloped her, causing her hair to dance with the tree and she knew He was with her.

A still, small voice whispered from deep inside, "I'm with you always. Do you remember when we met in the park?"

Rachel was awestruck, almost unable to speak. "Yes," she said, sitting upright.

"I told you I'd never leave. I'm always with you. But, sometimes you don't hear me over everything else. I love you, Rachel. I'm proud of you."

Overwhelmed with a feeling of love, Rachel buried her face in her hands and wept quietly. "Thank you," she said softly. "Thank you."

"I'd like to tell you more often," He said. "I just need you to listen. Remember, I am with you, always."

***

Strengthened and consoled, Rachel started the trek back toward her car. She felt enlightened and alive, as if a new energy had filled her soul. She couldn't wait to regroup with her family. But, as she made her way back toward the parking garage, she felt impressed to turn around and go the other way. Wanting to hurry to go get the kids, she continued forward only to feel her ears start to burn and the weight of the impression increase.

She stopped and looked at the lake, wondering if the feeling was just in her head. God had often inspired her to take action in some form, calling a friend, acknowledging a stranger, looking at a certain passage of scripture; but she had never been inspired to physically go somewhere. Was her mind playing tricks? After such a divine conversation, was her head trying to take it a step further?

While the impression felt different from the exchange she had just had with Holy Spirit, it still felt directed by something other than herself. She turned on her heels and headed east, finding herself on high alert as she scanned other pedestrians and her surroundings for a sign of some kind. Even with the consideration that she might be conjuring the impression in her own mind, she took each step with confidence realizing the importance of a divinely inspired assignment.

Just as she could see the black iron gate in the distance, indicating she was at the exit, she began to feel discouraged and disappointed. Had she missed something, she wondered? Or was she actually having delusions of grandeur. She had already received such a beautifully personal conversation with Holy Spirit, why would she think He would also send her on a Heavenly errand? Stopping near the exit, she said a silent prayer.

"What should I do, Lord? Did you really need me to go this way? Should I stay here or head back to go get the kids?"

A gentle answer seemed to rise from her heart, almost like a bubble, carrying the phrase, "Turn around."

Slightly miffed by her own confusion, Rachel wondered if she was misunderstanding or simply being tested. As she contemplated God's sense of humor, she pulled out her phone to text Pam. Rachel suddenly collided with a young woman going the other direction, also on her phone.

"Oh my gosh, you okay?" Rachel asked spinning around. "We hit hard."

The early 20-something girl gazed at her, looking annoyed. Rachel could tell she wanted to say something and braced herself for it to be unpleasant.

"Fine," the girl huffed and walked away.

Rachel stood there stunned. Having been physically turned around by the encounter, she  wondered if it was the reason for her deviation. She watched as the girl walked away and wondered if she should have handled it differently. Was she supposed to connect with that girl, minister to her? As she considered running after her, she spotted someone in the distance that made her instantly forget everything.

On a bench a mere 100-feet in front of her, Cody was sitting, staring out at the lake, looking glum. Rachel felt a gush of emotions rush in. Overcome with excitement to see her love unexpectedly, yet saddened that it took the Lord's help to arrange, she took a deep breath and watched him for a minute.

She didn't know what he was doing so far uptown. Looking at him from afar without his realization, she was actually able to see him. He was so strikingly handsome. In the midst of everything they had going on, she hadn't seen him clearly in a long time. She realized she had just been paying attention to their hurdles, issues, and responsibilities; she hadn't been looking at him.

He looked so depressed, it was hard to not race toward him and embrace him in a hug. But, at the same time she debated even approaching him, not wanting to impose on a private moment. She wondered what had him so down.

Grateful for the glimpse into a side of him that she wouldn't normally get to see, she offered thanks to God for the direction and opportunity. Just as she started toward him, he pushed up off the bench and headed for the exit with long, quick strides.

"Cody!" she shouted, trying to catch him.

He was unable to hear her with all of the evening traffic and people about. Unaware, he raced ahead, quickly on his way somewhere. She continued to run after him for a moment and then sank back, feeling like she wasn't going to catch him with all of the people between them she fished in her bag for her phone.

"Cody!" she shouted again one last time.

He turned around and spotted her among the crowds. As soon as he saw her, she noticed his countenance totally change. He lit up. There wasn't even a tinge of surprise on his face. It was as if he had been expecting her and was delighted to have finally found her.

He jogged toward her and swept her off her feet into a giant embrace.

"What are you doing here?" he asked, giving her a passionate kiss.

She felt herself melt into his arms. After a moment she was able to respond.

"I came for a prayer walk," she said. "And, I think, to find you."

He looked at her and smiled. She thought she could see tears in his eyes.

"God is good," he replied, seemingly awe struck. "Amazing."

Rachel agreed wholeheartedly. Her heart was singing with joy, but she was eager to understand what was going on with him. Why he was here, so far from the work site.

"Yeah," she agreed, giving him another hug. "I was blessed to get to spend some time with Holy Spirit this afternoon. He gently reminded me of all that we have…and how I'm not alone…even if I feel like it sometimes."

Cody took her hand and led her to a bench.

"Aw, Rach. I don't ever want you to feel alone…but, I get it," he said slowly. "He was with me this afternoon, too."

"Really? Were you here to pray?" Rachel asked.

"Yeah. I've really been struggling…with everything…," he said, trailing off. "I really needed His guidance. I was up this way to discuss the new project with Dan and on our way back we passed the park. I felt such a tug at my heart, I thought of you and your prayer walks and I just had to give it a try. I told him I'd see him back at work in a bit. Walking in here, I was instantly able to focus on all of the issues I've been having. I felt comforted as I brought it all to Him."

He shrugged and turned away.

"I know you've had some really incredible experiences with Holy Spirit, but mine have always been pretty subtle," he added. "I see God's blessings in my life, I feel support in my times of need, I've felt prompted to do things, but I've never actually heard His voice. He spoke with me today. He told me everything was going to be okay. I knew immediately I had to talk to you. But, I was still worried that we wouldn't have a good opportunity with the kids around. He told me to have faith. And, here you are."

He was quiet for a moment and then looked at her.

"There's something I need to talk to you about," he said.

It wasn't what Rachel had expected to hear after such an amazing experience with Holy Spirit and a heartfelt testimony. In her experience, those words never preceded good news.

She met his eyes and nodded. "Okay."

Cody looked ill, which made Rachel nervous.

"I wasn't honest when I told you how I got the job," he started. "Simone and I dated in college for a short time. That's why she remembered me. She remembered how into Arts and Craft woodwork I was from when we were together. I skimmed over that detail because I didn't want to worry you."

Rachel felt like someone was standing on her stomach. She could feel blood rushing to her cheeks, she didn't want to be angry with him. She wanted this serendipitous meeting to be romantic, not upsetting. Wanting the whole truth, Rachel worked to recall everything Cody had said about the job and Simone.

"Have you been in touch with her all these years and not mentioning it?" she asked.

Cody took her hands. "No, everything happened exactly like I said. I only left out the detail about us having dated. I feel like such a jerk because of it."

He paused and Rachel waited. She wasn't sure what to think. She knew she was angry, but she was unsure of how angry she should be. Even though she'd had her ideas about their relationship, she had never pictured a conversation like this.

"You've been warning me about her, trying to tell me you're uncomfortable since day one, and I haven't been listening," he said. "I felt nothing but friendship towards her, so I assumed it was mutual. But now, in retrospect, I can see what you were seeing, and there were red flags all along."

"Cody," Rachel said calmly, but feeling like she was going to explode inside. "Did something happen?"

He looked at her again, there was pain in his eyes. "Sort of."

Rachel felt another kick to her gut, and everything began to be veiled in a cloud of anger.

"Hear him out," a soft voice came from inside, helping her to not flip out.

He licked his lips nervously.

"After the tour and dinner last night, they drove us back to the work site. Everyone was tipsy from wine at dinner and being boisterous, friendly…just shy of drunk," he said with an uncomfortable laugh. "I didn't think anything when Simone came and sat down next to me. She was being particularly animated, touching my leg, my arm. It bothered me, like it always does, but she's just touchy-feely. So, again, I didn't think much of it. But, then, when we got back to the office, and everyone said good night, she kind of cornered me in the back office. No one else was around. I felt ridiculous, because it was intimidating in a way. I mean, she's half my size! She could tell it was making me anxious and she made some joke about it. I told her I had to go. Where she was standing blocked the exit. I had to get past her to get out."

Rachel could feel the heat building. In her gut, in her heart, she knew she trusted him, but his naivetey angered her. Had he just listened to her, *trusted her*, whatever else he was going to say would never have happened. Beyond that, it infuriated her that someone would take advantage of his kindness, loyalty, and virtue. A cool breeze whipped past, offering a momentary respite from her anger and enabling her to hear him out.

"Anyhow," he said, looking ashamed. "When I approached her, she didn't really move. I said, 'I'm leaving,' and tried to sort of squeeze past. She laughed at me and started to move, which made me relax and feel silly for being nervous. Then she said, 'Good night, Cody,' and went to give me what I thought were the little cheek kisses. I leaned forward to make it quick and easy — just wanting to get the heck out of there. But, she threw her arms around my neck and pulled me in for a real kiss. I was so shocked, I froze. I swear 500 thoughts raced through my mind all at once and while I don't think I kissed her back, I stood transfixed longer than I would have liked. Rachel, I'm so sorry. You warned me. I feel so guilty because I didn't shut it down before something like this happened. I feel like I've totally betrayed you. I love you more than anything on this earth and I never wanted to do anything to hurt you. I'm sorry for not being a better listener; for not being a better husband. You deserve someone who will defend your honor from the first whisperings of danger — not when he's in the clutches of it. Please forgive me."

Tears puddled in her eyes, but she didn't want to cry. She felt betrayed and didn't want to share her pain with him. Closing her eyes she knew she believed him, but still felt that the incident had caused a chink to their beautiful union.

"I'm not sure what to say," Rachel fumed. "This was an opportunity for you to prove your devotion to our family above things like work and superficial relationships, but you chose to ignore that. You chose appearance and work friendships over my wishes and it's done damage to our relationship."

She paused, unable to hold back the tears.

"I believe you, Cody. I do," she added. "It just makes me sad that you brushed off my warnings. This could have never happened had you just put up your defenses, like I asked. I wasn't telling you to quit or to not work with her — I asked you to be aware and cautious. Beyond that, you should have listened to yourself. I'm putting the pieces together in my memory and you knew what you were getting into. By omitting information that you knew would concern me, you lied. I saw the scripture passage you were reading the night before you started work...you knew you were entering a questionable situation. You knew you needed to walk with integrity to be safe."

He looked at her.

"Someone who walks with integrity will be safe," he quoted. "But one who follows a crooked path will fall into the pit. Proverbs 10:9."

He shook his head, disappointed in himself.

Another breeze blew past carrying with it a shift; a reminder of her own questionable behavior. Looking at Cody, she could see her own self-mirrored in him. She hadn't been exactly upright in her dealings with Tom. If he wasn't decent and strong, Rachel could have found herself in a similar, if not worse position. Suddenly, she completely understood how this happened. Her heart softened and she felt a wave of remorse. She was so grateful that nothing worse had happened — with either of them.

Shifting, she turned to face him. She gently brushed her hand against his face and he closed his eyes. She could see the grief on his face for hurting her.

"We just both need to do better," she said. "Our partnership, our family, our life in Christ, takes priority over everything. If we ever find ourselves moving away from that, we need to talk about it and change course immediately, you know? We can't take this lightly. We've been so blessed. We can't take it for granted."

A tear rolled down Cody's cheek and he opened his eyes to meet her gaze.

"I love you," he said. "Do you forgive me?"

"Yes," she said giving him a hug. "I love you, too."

Cody gave her a kiss and held her hands. For a moment they sat together in silence, enveloped in the soft evening breeze.

"I talked to Him about some other stuff, too," he said, breaking the silence. "About being here in the city, this job…"

"Okay," Rachel coaxed, her nerves on edge as she anticipated what he was about to say.

"I think it's time we go back to Collinsville," he said.

Not aware that she had been holding her breath, Rachel exhaled with relief and smiled.

"Me too," she agreed giving him another hug. "Me too."

\*\*\*

Rachel felt peaceful and light, like a weight had been removed, as she went to pick up the kids. There had been three relationships reconciled that afternoon: the one between her and her Heavenly Father, the one between her and Cody, and the one with herself. She finally felt at ease. The spiteful, lonely voices in her mind were quiet and she could finally see her situation clearly. She was blessed beyond measure.

Cody had finally decided he had pushed hard enough. He described it as, "Pushing a boulder up a hill, where, when he got to the top, was only going to be met with cocktails, touchy-feely French girls, and more boulders."

Rachel had laughed, but then realizing the truth in the ridiculous illustration had given him a consolidating hug. She knew he loved the work, it was everything else that ruined it.

"It's not my scene," he conceded. "I'm going to talk to Dan today. I won't put in notice outright, but I'll explain my situation and see if there's any opportunity to work from home."

"Are you going to tell him about Simone?" Rachel had asked.

Unsure, Cody shook his head.

"I'll only tell him what I need to. Even after what she did, I feel sorry for her. I don't want to get her in trouble. I just don't want to work with her."

Rachel had considered the situation on her walk back to the car. In the end, she realized she had sympathy for Simone, too. Knowing Cody was loyal and dedicated to her and the kids, enabled her to see Simone on her own terms, and it was sad.

Rachel discovered after only a couple months of dating, Cody had broken it off with Simone. She had always been a negative influence, pressuring him to go to parties, skip church, and do things that made him uncomfortable; he eventually got fed up. But, Rachel supposed it was the fact

Cody left her that had her pining for him all these years later. He was the one that got away. Rachel wondered if his having a family made him an even more enticing challenge.

To have such a carnal, superficial view of life and love, made Rachel feel bad for her. She was grateful for her own understanding of the Lord's love, the role of family, and His plan of salvation. She prayed that Simone might receive the same knowledge someday, and in the meantime stay away from her husband.

"I pray you save her from heartache," Rachel prayed. "I can't imagine walking through life without you. And, please protect Cody."

As she arrived at her dad's she raced up the stairs.

"They're eager to see you," Pam said, greeting her at the door. "We had a great day. It's so fun to see Sky's little personality emerge! But, I think we wore them out with too much fun in the sun."

Rachel walked in to find Sky curled up on the couch watching her iPad and Slater happily bouncing in the chair from Mrs. Pierson right next to her. As soon as Sky noticed Rachel she smiled and got up to toddle over.

"Mama!" she said.

"Aw, sweet girl," Rachel said picking her up and giving her a kiss. "Sounds like you had a full day. Are you ready to go home and see Daddy?"

She nodded and returned her attention to her iPad.

Slater bounced enthusiastically as Rachel set down Skylark to pick him up. Covering him in kisses, she felt an overwhelming sense of appreciation for the Lord's plan. She had been so distracted by the need for attention, wealth, career, and the like, she had lost sight of the big picture.

"This is what it's all about," she said to Pam.

"Oh, honey, ain't it the truth? You'll still feel that way even when their 20."

*** 

Rachel was just pulling the kids out of the bath when Cody walked in to the hotel room.

"Hello?" he shouted.

"We're in the bathroom. How'd the conversation go with Dan?"

He came in and leaned against the sink.

"How do you think it went?" he asked, his old, familiar grin returning to his face.

"Well, I'm assuming it went well," she replied, handing him Skylark wrapped in an oversized towel. "I haven't seen that smug look for months."

He gave Skylark a kiss on the forehead. "How was your day, little lady? Did you have fun with Grandpa Jo and Pam?"

Sky nodded and started to wriggle wanting down.

"Cody!" Rachel exclaimed with an exasperated laugh. "I'm waiting. We all are. Tell us what happened."

He clapped his hands energetically and took Slater from Rachel.

"Let me preface this by saying, I know this makes me look like a real jerk for not having approached Dan sooner."

Rachel tilted her head and gave him a twisted smile. "Go on."

"When I got back to work, it was almost the end of the day. I asked him if he had a few minutes to talk and we went into his office. I explained being in the city wasn't working out for my family and I needed to head back to Collinsville. I told him I was happy to continue to consult, but I needed to be based at home."

"And, what'd he say?" Rachel asked, surprised by Cody's frankness.

"He said, 'no problem.' Do you believe that? Who knows if it would've been the same response if I had asked a couple of months ago, but today it was, 'No problem.' He said we'd need to figure out the exact logistics, but that I'm an invaluable member to the team and he wanted to keep me on. To be honest, Rach, the simplicity of the conversation actually left me a little nauseous. It made me review the past few months, and question if I should've done things differently. Regardless, I'm still employed and we can head back home."

Rachel grabbed Skylark and began to dance around, causing her to giggle uncontrollably. She embraced Cody and Slater in a family hug and they all jumped around excitedly.

Rachel stopped and caught her breath.

"Incredible," she sighed. "Family prayer?"

Cody nodded and together they expressed their love and gratitude.

# CHAPTER ELEVEN
# HOMEWARD BOUND

"Thank you so much for everything," Rachel said handing District Attorney Pierson a box of his favorite cupcakes.

"Well, isn't that thoughtful…although my waistline doesn't thank you," he said laughing. "Tom did all the heavy lifting. I just leant my name."

She smiled.

"Yes, well, if you could reiterate my gratitude to him…," she said trailing off. "I didn't realize he was taking a vacation after DC."

"I'm not sure he did either," Matt replied, preparing to head into another meeting. "I'll be sure to tell him when he returns."

Rachel smiled and waved good-bye making her exit. As she approached the elevators, she recalled her last visit to District Attorney Pierson's office. The feeling of love and gratitude, standing in this same spot, holding her sweet Skylark, and knowing God's hand was supporting her in their efforts to do the right thing. Still unsure whether Skylark would stay with them or be returned to her birthmother, Rachel had felt surrounded by good people, truly willing to help her get to the bottom of it. Those two were again, Tom and Matt.

She really did wish she had the opportunity to express her gratitude to Tom in person. She knew he was well aware he had gone above and beyond, but it would have been nice to tell him. She told herself it was okay to let it go. It was the right thing to let it go…to let him go. She felt a sudden pang of guilt, wondering if she had enlisted his help under false pretenses. She hoped he didn't feel used. Her heart would be eternally grateful to him for more than he would ever know.

Not up for a long trek, she flagged down a cab and gave the driver the address for the clinical trial. She couldn't wait to see Susan. Less than a week into the trial and off her old medications, Susan looked like a new person. Her color had returned, the twinkle in her eyes was sparked, and, best of all, her personality had returned and then some. Filled with hope and faith, Susan was brimming with energy and excitement and it was wonderful to witness.

The trial was being held at Dr. Hamming's home office. An old brick building in the East Village covered in vines, it felt more like a therapist's office or a friend's home for tea. As the cab pulled up to the curb, Rachel noticed a few leaves flutter to the ground from the large Maple tree out front. She could feel fall in the air and it was a welcomed change. A soft breeze greeted her as she exited the cab and Rachel swayed with it as she walked to the door

"Hey, girl!" Susan sang as Rachel entered.

Sprawled out on a leather recliner, smart phone in one hand, an ice water in the other, Susan looked as though she could be lounging on a beach somewhere if it wasn't for the IV in her arm. Rachel took a seat on the coffee table next to her and rubbed her leg.

"You look great!" she said. "How're you feeling?"

"Oh, Rachel, my girl, I couldn't feel better," Susan said happily. "Dr. Hamming is just incredible. He's truly a brilliant man. And, while I still have a ways to go, the progress we've seen just pulling me off the other medications has been huge."

"I'm so glad to hear it," Rachel said. She looked out the window to the busy sidewalk. A building down from a popular cafe and bakery, people milled about out front eating treats and slurping on iced coffees. She was tempted to get something for the both of them to share but thought better of it, knowing the treatment made Susan's stomach sensitive.

"Can you believe that we both get to head back to *Collinsville*?" Susan asked excitedly.

"No," Rachel said honestly. "This whole summer has just been such a whirlwind. It's held some truly amazing gifts, but on a whole it's been pretty trying. I'm ready for autumn back home."

"Mmmm, Pumpkin Spice Cheesecake Yogurt with a hot cup of coffee from *Cali's*," Susan tossed out.

"The red, orange, and golden yellow leaves dancing in the crisp breeze on late afternoon prayer walks in the park," Rachel added.

"Doris and Vera's apple pie made with fresh apples from their tree for the church's Harvest Festival," Susan said.

Rachel laughed. "Someone's hungry."

"Oh, girl, you have no idea," she said smiling sheepishly. "That's the only negative. Dr. Hamming has me on the Mediterranean diet and I'm missing my highly processed treats."

"Well, I bet Vera and Doris would be happy to accommodate you," Rachel said.

Susan looked at her and laughed.

"No, they wouldn't," they both said in unison.

"Anyway," Rachel said a little distracted. "I'm looking forward to heading back. We leave tomorrow morning. How about you?"

"We'll head back Saturday," Susan replied. "John'll be leading Sunday service."

"I can't wait to get back to church," Rachel sighed. "It feels like forever since we've been. I need to be 'spiritually fed.'"

Susan smiled at the Pastor Bishop reference.

"I'm looking forward to it, too," she agreed. "We'll be back to the city every Wednesday for check-ins, but we plan to make those day trips."

"I'd be happy to take you for some of those," Rachel offered, unexpectedly. "While I'm eager to get home...I've remembered why I love the city and to get to support you while also keeping a connection to this unique place would be great."

"It is a special place," Susan agreed. "I'll take you up on that some time. It'll be fun to be out here during Christmas time. Oh, and the hot chocolate from *Max Brenner's*; that'll be a must come the holidays."

Giggling, Rachel asked, "This has to be a good sign, don't you think? Something's obviously working if your appetite's back, right?"

"Not a minute to soon," Susan agreed. "My cheeks were starting to look sallow and sucked in. I look forward to doing what's necessary to regain my girly curves!"

Rachel laughed and stood to leave.

"I'll see you at church on Sunday?" she asked.

"You know it, girl," Susan replied holding Rachel's hand. "Thank you for checking in on me. It means the world to me.

By the way, I've been trying to think of something nice to do for the Pierson boys. Any ideas?"

Rachel gave her hand a squeeze. "Let's just send them your trial discharge declaring you cancer-free."

Susan beamed with her familiar Cheshire grin. "Sounds like a plan."

Rachel gave her a hug and headed towards the door.

"Give those little angels of yours a big hug and kiss from me," Susan said. "I can't wait to have the energy again to watch them!"

Rachel nodded and made her way back outside. Greeted by another draft of autumn air, she decided to take a walk through the East Village toward NYU. She loved the neighborhood. It was old school New York. Quaint, charming, historic, and cultured, it was everything she loved about the city, with just enough grit to make it fun.

She had a couple of last minute errands before picking-up the kids from her dad's, but had time to enjoy the journey. Along the short walk, she window-shopped boutiques, stopping to take pictures of the best window displays to send to Maddie for inspiration at *Cali's*. As she approached Washington Square Park, she could hear discordant, but lively music. There was a classical pianist, a drumming group playing on plastic buckets, and a dance troupe performing to a pop song.

Meandering through the park she watched the performances and observed the many college students milling about. It seemed a lifetime, yet not that long ago, that she was a student herself meeting friends, doing homework, and people watching in this exact place. Considering how far she had come, both temporally and spiritually made her heart leap. She was grateful for where she was now. It was all a blessing from Him.

From a few feet away a woman started toward her.

"Excuse me, miss," she said. "Do you know how in the world to get to Vanderbilt Hall?"

Rachel smiled.

"The School of Law?" she asked, making sure they had the same place.

"Yes, my husband and I have been going in circles," she replied, exasperated. "We're supposed to be meeting our son for dinner."

"Yes, I know where it is. I'll walk you over there."

The woman looked relieved and waved her husband over.

"I'm Lila and this is Don," she said extending a hand. "Thank you for your help."

"It's just right up here," Rachel said, pointing to her alma mater. "You were really close."

"Oh, I don't know how you kids do it," Lila replied. "We've been here a handful of times and get lost every single time. I don't understand how you all aren't constantly lost."

Rachel felt a rush of air whip around her and stillness in her heart as she considered the woman's words.

"Oh, it's easy to get lost in Manhattan," Rachel agreed. "I was lost recently myself, but I found a guide to show me the way."

Pointing across the street to a stately brick building, she said, "There you go."

Lila and her husband thanked Rachel and rushed on their way. Rachel stopped and ruminated on the exchange. She had gotten so lost by trying to find her own way. Distracted by petty fears, lured by worldly desires, and forgetful of spiritual needs, she went astray. Finding herself lost, it had just taken the Lord's hand to help her get back on track.

Taking a seat on a bench, she watched the students coming in and out. She closed her eyes and listened to the distant, indistinct chatter, city traffic, street musicians, and muffled sounds of birds chirping and the breeze rustling the trees. The city had been a great place for many seasons of her life. This summer, it had served a purpose. In the end, she had come to remember what a special place it was. Like an old friend, the city had welcomed her openly, and in return Rachel had rekindled a flame for it that she had let dwindle.

"Thank you, Lord, for the time here," she whispered.

In a way she had received an opportunity to revisit experiences, feelings and emotions from her past that would allow her to move forward back home in Collinsville. Since becoming a mom she had felt out of sorts, as though she had lost a bit of herself. The daydreams about her time as a New York City lawyer, viewing the role sometimes as more important than her role as mom, had left her wondering *what if.* As Cody toiled in city, far from them in Collinsville, she had found herself building up the time in her life when money was never an issue. It was easy to never be content in her present moments when considering how green she considered things in her past and what could have been her future.

She was leaving the city with a very good understanding of what could have been and a grateful heart for what was her reality. A soft, cool gush of air encircled her and Rachel closed her eyes. Holy Spirit was always with her. He was always with Cody. They both just needed to stop and pay attention. With His counsel they would never lose their way.

\*\*\*

"I received a text from Jaime," Cody said out of the blue as they drove to meet her dad, Pam and the kids.

"Jaime in El Salvador?" Rachel asked, confused. "The guy from your team that was picked up by immigration?"

"Yeah," he said sadly.

"What'd it say?"

"He needs help. He's worried about his family. They're still here." Cody turned to Rachel and shrugged. He added, "I need to do something."

Rachel's heart felt heavy. After her experience this summer playing single parent to Sky and Slater, she couldn't bear to think of Jaime's wife on her own, unsure of her husband's return, struggling to shelter and feed two young kids.

"We have to do something," she agreed.

"I should've done something before," Cody said. "I feel really responsible. I don't know. Maybe I was scared to get involved. No, if I'm being honest, I was too caught up in my own stuff...I should've done better."

Rachel patted his arm. "It's not your fault, Cody. But, I totally understand. Did Jamie ask for anything specific? Do you know what kind of help he needs?"

"He wanted me to check on them," he said heavily. "He said his wife, Ana, is angry at him and not responding to his calls."

"That's terrible," Rachel said with a sigh. "Where do they live? Should we go now? Tomorrow morning?"

"She works," he said. "So, I was thinking after dinner tonight we could grab a gift card to a grocery store and then stop by to see what else they might need."

"Sounds like a plan."

For a fleeting moment Rachel silently asked herself why they could never catch a break; why there always had to be drama. Instantly regretful, she requested forgiveness for the lack of sympathy. She really did feel terrible for them and wanted to help, she was also just eager to get home to Collinsville.

They found a parking spot right in front of her dad's building and Cody turned to look at her.

"I know it seems like we always have something awful going on," Cody said as if he could hear her thoughts. "The first thought I had when I got the text this afternoon, was *really? More bad stuff?* Then, a little voice reminded me…we are His hands on Earth and it's up to us to care for His people. *This* is what it's all about, you know?"

He bit his lip for a moment, thinking, and added, "I'm not saying that I wouldn't appreciate a little staycation or something, but it's important that we make this stuff a priority."

"You're 100 percent right," she agreed.

When they got upstairs, it was as if the kids knew they would be leaving the close proximity to Pam and Joe soon. Both held a firm grip on their grandparents, uninterested in going to mom or dad.

As they all walked to the restaurant a few blocks away, Rachel enjoyed the freedom by holding Cody's hand.

"You're leaving right before the beautiful fall weather," Joe said.

"I know, I can feel the seasons transitioning," Rachel admitted. "Central Park is stunning on a crisp, fall day…but, I do believe Collinsville has the city beat for autumnal charm."

Joe made a face like he was going to try to dispute the claim, but then sighed.

"It's true," he said with a laugh. "It's been nice having you all so close. You can't blame an old man for trying to extend the stay."

"Aw, Dad," Rachel said. "This summer's been a great reminder of how much the city has to offer. It's been great being out here. With you guys, Cody's work, and Susan's weekly doctor appointments, we'll be visiting way more often. Plus, while Collinsville has you beat for fall, Christmas in Manhattan is pretty dreamy."

"Okay, so it's a deal," Pam jumped into the conversation. "Thanksgiving at your house? Christmas at ours?"

Everyone laughed.

"Deal," Rachel agreed.

***

After dinner, while her dad and Pam coddled Sky and Slater avoiding the good-bye, Rachel ran across the street to a *Walgreens*. She picked up a handful of gift cards for groceries and necessities. She paused at a card for dinner and a movie. Unsure of Jaime's family's exact situation, she thought better of it. If they were tight on money, a gift card for entertainment would be thoughtful; if they had no money and didn't know where their next meal was coming from, it would be a frivolity. She figured the money would better spent on basic needs.

On the way to the register, she grabbed a card and envelope to hold everything. In a way she felt guilty. She and Cody had talked about money. The job in the city had been a result of them wanting more — more stability, more comfort, more opportunity. But, when she looked at her situation in relation to something dire, she was embarrassed for wanting anything more than they already had.

As she made her way back across the street, she looked at her family. They were congregated on the curb in front of an Italian restaurant Rachel went to as a kid with her mom and dad when they were together. The view made her feel overwhelmingly blessed. The past few years had been an outpouring of love and generosity from God.

While there had been plenty of challenges along the way, He had given her Cody, Skylark, Slater, Collinsville, *Cali's,* and a renewed relationship with her own dad. When she added it all up, any desire for more worldly possessions seemed ridiculous and trite. She decided she was determined to help Jaime's family anyway she could, in the hopes of sharing what she had so generously been blessed with.

"All set?" Cody asked as she approached.

"Yep," she replied with a peck on his cheek.

Giving her dad and Pam a hug, she took Skylark into her arms and got ready to leave.

"Thanks for all of your help these past few weeks," she said. "Our time here wouldn't have been the same without your support. I'm going to miss having you guys so close."

"We sure are, too," Pam said. "It's been a really fun summer for us. We'll schedule some time to come up your way soon. And, I wasn't joking about the holidays. If you're up for it, we'd love to host Christmas."

"It's a wonderful plan," Rachel replied. "We'll look forward to having you for Thanksgiving. "

Skylark began to rub her eyes.

"Well, Princess," Joe said, putting his arm over Rachel's shoulders. "You better get this little gal home to bed. Thanks for dinner. Do you remember the last time we were here with your mom?"

Rachel thought about it. "No," she said. "I remember coming here as a family, but I don't recall any specifics."

"You were probably 6," he recalled, quietly. "Yeah, you were 6, because I left not too long after. It was a nice dinner, though. I think we were kicking off the new school year. You had just started 1st grade and were the most precocious little thing. The night always stood out in my mind, because it was the way things should have been — us, together, as a happy family. Your mom was relaxed, appreciating a meal out, you were energized talking about your first day, and I was full of love seeing you two enjoy yourselves. Things had already been tumultuous before that, and they got worse after, but it was a nice dinner."

Hearing him reminisce, Rachel wished she remembered, but she didn't.

"It sounds nice," Rachel said, wistfully. "I find it surprising that being back in the city hasn't unlocked more memories of mom. I hadn't thought about it until now, but I would've expected to feel her here more...at least more than I do in Collinsville."

Joe tilted his fedora back, considering Rachel's confession.

"You know, princess, she was always an angel among us," he said. "There's no place here special enough for her spirit."

"But, mom loved the city," Rachel countered.

"She loved her own romanticized version of the city," he said. "I always wished I was able to see it through her eyes. When you were a kid, you could see what she did. But, when you feel her spirit now, you know it's not from anywhere around these parts."

Rachel smiled and gave her dad a hug. "I love that," she whispered. "Thank you. We'll see you guys soon."

\*\*\*

Both kids were asleep within minutes of the drive. Rachel looked at her phone, playing navigator and getting excited at the prospect of helping out someone in need.

"It says we should be there in 20 minutes," she said softly.

"Thank you for doing this tonight," Cody said. "I know we should be putting the kids to bed. I just really do feel responsible. I'd like to help any way we can."

"Of course," she agreed. "Did you let Jaime know we were going by?"

"I tried. The text bounced…it came back undelivered."

"Oh," Rachel replied, thinking. "Well, let's see what they need and we'll keep trying to let him know. I just know if it was me away from you guys…I'd be panicked."

She paused. "If for some reason we are ever separated…I don't care if you're mad at me, you better pick up the phone."

Cody laughed. "Deal."

Pulling up to a large brick apartment complex, Cody turned to Rachel. "I didn't think about this part. We can't go up together, because we can't leave the kids."

"Let me go," Rachel offered. "It's late. I think it will be much less threatening to have me knock at their door at 9 p.m. than you."

"You're right," he agreed, giving her a kiss. "Sorry so much of this is falling on you."

"I'm happy to do it."

Cody squeezed her hand and gave her another kiss. "Be cautious. Jaime's a good guy, so I assume his wife is decent, too; but you never know."

Rachel walked to the front of the building and wiggled the door. Locked. Scanning the building's entry panel, she looked at the buzzer next to Ana Ramirez, Jaime's name was listed too. She debated what to do. If she announced her arrival, Ana might not be interested in letting her up. Figuring it was worth a shot, she hit the buzzer of another random tenant.

"Yeah?" asked a tired voice.

"I'm sorry, I forgot my key, can you let me in?"

The door hummed as it unlocked and Rachel made her way inside. The building was old, like most buildings in New York; but this one was showing its age from years of neglect. There was a caustic scent in the air that she couldn't place, reminiscent of rotting food and soiled diapers. Noticing a few trash bags set in the hallway, she figured her nose was accurate. The unsettling sounds of a baby wailing down the hall, made Rachel hesitate before climbing the dark staircase.

As she reached the third floor, the lighting was better. The hallway, clear of debris and stinky trash bags, was slightly more inviting. Navigating toward 3F, Rachel took a deep breath and knocked softly. She tried to recall the age of their children. She knew they were young, but probably not as young as Sky and Slater.

After a minute, she knocked a little louder.

She saw a shadow pass behind the peephole.

"Hello?" Rachel said softly. "My husband worked with Jaime. I've brought you…"

The door cracked open and half a woman's face appeared under the chain.

"Did he send you to check-in on us?" she asked angrily.

"No, well," Rachel stammered not wanting to lie, but nervous to tell the truth. "Not really. I've brought you a gift."

The woman unlatched the door and opened it enough that Rachel was able to see her whole face, but little else.

"A gift?" she asked, skeptical. "A gift because my husband's gone?"

Rachel suddenly felt silly. Was that what she was offering?

"No," she said, feeling a wave of sympathy. "No. It's just a little something because it's hard to manage on your own. And, until he gets back home, we'd like to help."

Ana reached out and took the letter from Rachel. Opening it, she pulled out the gift cards and nodded.

"This is very helpful, thank you," she said softly. "I normally wouldn't accept charity, but as you said...it can be hard to manage on your own."

Rachel was so relieved. "What do you need? What else can we do to help?"

Ana smiled. "These will get us through the month, thank you. I've been able to keep up with all of the major bills...it's just staples, like diapers and healthy food, I've been worried about. I can get by on peanut butter and jelly, but the kids need more. You know?"

"What about next month?" Rachel asked.

"As long as I keep the same hours at work, it'll be the same," she replied.

Suddenly a small hand wrapped around Ana's leg.

"Gilbert," she said exasperated. "You're supposed to be asleep."

"The baby's noisy," he said quietly. "I can't sleep."

"We're all in one room," Ana explained to Rachel. "It has its drawbacks."

"Mama? Who's the lady?" he inquired.

"She's a friend of daddy's," Ana said, trying to scoot him toward the hall.

"Is daddy coming home?"

"Ah, Gilbert, to bed," Ana directed in frustration. "I'll be in shortly."

The little boy obediently sulked off to bed. Ana turned back to Rachel.

"How do you explain deportation to a 4-year-old?" she asked with a heavy shrug.

Rachel wasn't sure.

"Anyhow, I really do appreciate the gift cards. Thank you," Ana added, preparing to close the door.

Rachel felt a burning in her chest. She knew the Lord wanted her to make a deeper connection. *Don't let her go*, her heart implored.

"Can I get your number?" Rachel asked, putting her hand up to gently block the door from closing. "We live upstate, but are in the city fairly often. I'd like to stay in touch. Would that be okay?"

Ana considered the question longer than Rachel would have liked.

"I guess that'd be all right," she finally said, holding out her hand.

Rachel handed over her phone hoping it was what Ana was expecting. She took it and knowingly entered her number.

"Don't call during the day," she said, nervously. "A text would be okay, but if I forget to turn off my ringer...I can't have anything jeopardize my job."

"Got it," Rachel agreed. "After 5 p.m., okay?"

"Yes, thanks."

"Well, Ana, I'm glad I caught you," Rachel said stepping back, allowing her space to close the door. "It was nice to meet you...and Gilbert."

"I never got your name," Ana said softly.

"I'm Rachel. Rachel Brooks. My husband's name is Cody."

"Thank you, Rachel."

Rachel smiled and made her way back down the hall. As she approached the stairs, the lights flickered back on, illuminating her way down and leaving her with a much better impression of the building than when she entered.

"How'd it go?" Cody asked as Rachel settled into the car.

"Good. She was pretty guarded at first, but I think we ended on a good note," she explained. "She was appreciative. She needed the help."

"Would it of been better to give her cash?"

"No, I think what we gave her was perfect. I know it was hard for her to accept help. But, I think it was easier to take gift cards...they feel more like a present than a handout, you know?"

"That makes sense," he agreed. "How'd you leave it? What else does she need?"

Rachel contemplated the question.

"She needs the same thing next month," she said. "But, what she really needs is her husband home. Cody, how do we make that happen?"

He coughed quietly, taken back by the question.

"I don't know that we have any role in that," he replied, uncertain. "Why? Did you have something in mind?"

"No, not really," she conceded. "But...isn't Jaime an expert at Arts and Craft style? I remember hearing in one of my real estate cases years ago that you could legally hire a foreign employee, if you could prove they were an expert in something...and that there weren't a bunch of U.S. candidates with the same level of expertise."

Cody was quiet for a moment.

"I think with all my personal research over the years, looking for help on various commissioned pieces, and with Jaime's resume — I mean, he helped restore the Roycroft estate in Buffalo — he could absolutely be considered an expert."

"How do we hire him?" Rachel asked getting excited.

"I'll talk to Dan," Cody said. "Jaime was an integral part of my team. It's been apparent the other guys aren't up to snuff since he's been gone. If the group went through the proper legal channels to bring him back, it would be a good investment for them. I'm sure I could convince them of that."

Rachel felt a tension release from her shoulders and scooted down in her seat relaxing.

"I'm excited to head home tomorrow," she said.

"I'll talk to Dan first thing and then we'll be on our way."

***

Rachel scanned the hotel room for any overlooked socks, toiletries, and precious trinkets that could result in mid-trip meltdowns. With all of their stuff out, the space recaptured its sophisticated, understated beauty and felt serene.

Looking out over the Hudson, Rachel was taken with the beauty of the morning. Picture book, puffy white clouds floated low in a pristine blue sky. A cool, early autumn breeze pushed everything northward, making Rachel eager to do the same.

"Lord, thank you for the time here. Thank you for watching over us. I'm grateful for the opportunity to return home stronger and more united than when we arrived."

As Rachel exited the lobby, she could see Cody and the kids double-parked, waiting for her. Racing to the car, she got in just as the hotel's doorman was motioning for Cody to move along. Cody waved and pulled forward as Rachel secured her seatbelt.

"Mama!" Skylark exclaimed.

"You ready for a road trip, luv bug?" Rachel asked rubbing her head over the back of the car seat.

Slater was happily kicking his legs and chattering to himself. Rachel handed Sky her favorite electronic book toy and she quickly opened the first page to hear "Old McDonald."

Cody laughed. "You know we're going to be listening to that for the next two hours."

"No…," Rachel countered. "We get the occasional break with 'Twinkle, Twinkle Little Star.' So, how'd the conversation go with Dan?"

"Not great," he admitted. "It's not that he didn't see the value in Jaime; it's that they're a team of independent investors. They all want to be nimble and keep their flexibility…not have the liability of full-time employees. The entire team's made up of independent contractors. When the job's done, Dan, or any of the other partners, have the ability to walk away unhindered."

"Oh," Rachel replied disappointed. "That's a bummer."

"I know. But, don't give up. Let's keep thinking about what else we can do. I know we'll come up with something."

\*\*\*

Driving through the tunnel of trees leading into Collinsville, Rachel's heart beat faster. The fading green foliage still offered a dense passage into town, and she was grateful to see it again, before the fall colors emerged.

As they rolled down their gravel drive, approaching the house, Cody took Rachel's hand in his and gave it a squeeze.

"We're home," he whispered.

"Home!" Skylark repeated excitedly, echoing Rachel's own internal sentiment perfectly.

# CHAPTER TWELVE
## THE PARK

Susan took a deep breath and touched at an errant tear with a tissue. Her blue eyes sparkled damp with emotion and ignited with passion for her desire to lift up every woman in the chapel.

"What I'm saying is…if we don't look after *ourselves*, who's going to care for all of those we nurture and love each day? Sure, it's easy to push off routine exams. There's always something else more pressing. There are always seemingly more important things to do. As women, it comes naturally to make sure everyone around us, everyone we love, has their needs taken care of before our own. Our husbands, our kids, our brothers and sisters, our parents, our friends, our neighbors, our church family, those we volunteer to serve, those we work for philanthropically, and those disadvantaged groups we hear about in a *PBS documentary* or *public radio* segment, tend to get more of our time and concern than our own health and wellbeing."

The audience of women quietly chuckled in agreement with Susan.

Rachel dabbed at her eyes, overcome with emotion for how amazing it was to see Susan on the stage healthy, happy and vibrant again. Advocating for women's health, utilizing her community position to urge for routine mammograms and other exams, her experience had come full circle. Rachel found it to be the perfect platform for her ministry, humor, tenderness, and personal story, and she couldn't be more excited to see her on stage.

"All right, ladies," Susan shouted. "Let's talk boobies!"

A roar of applause erupted and Susan glowed. It was as though His divine light was shining right through her. Rachel only half listened to the next 45 minutes of Susan's seminar, spending much of the time in and out of prayer, thanking God for His goodness...for healing her dear friend. At the break, Rachel headed to the side of the stage. Clapping as Susan approached, she embraced her.

"You're amazing...turning such a challenge in your life into a tool to help others," Rachel praised. "What an important message that we all need to hear."

"God's amazing," Susan countered. "I'm just leveraging my platform for His message. He wants His daughters to remember themselves. We've got to remember *us* to be able to give our best. I forgot and as a result was unable to serve the way I wanted to. I was unable to love the way I wanted to. And, I was unable to be the best *me* while I battled to get healthy. That was the worst part."

Rachel gave her another hug. "I love you, Susan."

"I love you, girl. Oh, hey, I almost forgot. I've been so busy gearing up for this seminar series. I received a letter from Tom."

Rachel's stomach did a flip-flop. "Tom, Tom? NY Tom?"

"Uh-huh," Susan replied excited. "When I got released from the clinical trial, I sent him and Matt my 'clean bill of health' with a thank-you note and some goodies. He wrote back and I thought you should see it."

Susan handed Rachel a precisely folded letter on Tom's business letterhead. She recognized the paper instantly.

*Dear Susan,*

*Thank you very much for the tasty cheesecake yogurt. I can without a doubt say that was the first time I've received a frozen treat in the mail.*

Rachel looked up from the letter. "How in the world did you…?" she started to ask. "Lots and lots of dry ice, but don't get caught up in the details," Susan replied. "It gets good. Keep reading."

*Above all though, thank you for sending a note to let us know that you are in good health. It is wonderful to know that we were able to play a small role in your recovery.*

*As Rachel can attest to, I've lived a very privileged life. Most everything has been given or come easily to me. I've taken a lot for granted. And, as a result it has been difficult to find joy and meaning in life. Getting to use my talents and leverage my position to help you get the medical help you needed brings meaning to my life. The fact that it worked, brings exceeding joy. So, thank you for trusting our little team.*

*Helping you, and formerly helping with the adoption of Skylark, has impacted my life greatly. I have been seeking out pro bono opportunities to help others that are struggling or in need and I'm enjoying it immensely.*

*I am grateful to you for taking care of Rachel. She will always hold a special place in my heart. I've learned a lot from you Collinsville folk over the past two years. You all have this countenance — this*

*special light — that I don't see much anywhere else. I*
*believe it has something to do with God and the* Bible,
*but I hope to someday understand it all a little better.*
*If you're ever back in the city, I'd be honored to take*
*you for a cup of coffee. If Pastor Bishop's available,*
*please bring him too (I have lots of questions).*

*Thank you again.*

*Sincerely,*

*Tom Pierson*

Rachel felt a wave of emotion hit her chest, centered right at her heart. She slowly folded the letter back up as she worked to hold back the tears pushing to stream down her face. She handed it to Susan and cleared her throat.

"What a nice letter," she said softly.

Susan grabbed Rachel and gave her a tight hug.

"I cried ugly tears when I read it, sweetie," she said with a laugh. "You're doing amazingly well."

With the recognition, Rachel's emotions burst through and she wept tears of joy and love.

"Oh, Susan, you and Pastor Bishop have to meet with him," she cried, grabbing Susan's hand.

"We're meeting him tomorrow after I go check-in with Dr. Hamming."

"Thank you," she said. "This is so exciting. I know the Lord will do amazing things in his life. He already is."

"Oh, girl, I'm just excited he came to me. That boy's already been a miracle worker, imagine what he'll do with God on his side."

\*\*\*

"He's going to start crawling any day...our boy's crazy strong," Cody said handing Slater to Rachel.

"*And*, he needs to compete with his big sis," Rachel replied, stroking Sky's hair as she hugged her leg. "I'm pretty sure this precocious little gal started crawling at 6 months on the dot."

Rachel covered Slater in kisses, relishing his bubbly giggles.

"How was the seminar?" Cody asked.

"It was so good to see Susan on stage healthy, vibrant, filled with Holy Spirit and completely energized by her new commitment to women's health," Rachel replied excited. "I love her passion…and a lot of what she said really resonated. I know I've neglected appointments because I've had too much going on, and I can only imagine it'll get worse as the kids get older and more active. I know going through this experience with her, and her personal insights from the seminar will help me remember the value in taking care of myself."

Cody threw his arm over her shoulders and pulled her in to his chest. "Yes, please. We need you. Right, buddy?" he asked Slater.

Rachel gave him a kiss and set Slater in his walker. "So, enough chit-chat," she teased. "What'd Jaime say?"

With a sly smile, Cody handed her his phone. "He just texted. Take a look."

Rachel looked at Cody's phone. The green text bubble floated mid-screen, notifying them that he would indeed take the job. His family was eager to make the move to Collinsville.

Rachel's feet leapt from the ground. Over the past few months she and Ana had formulated a real friendship. Rachel's quick check-ins, friendly texts, and snail mail letters bearing words of support and stacks of gift cards had evolved into thoughtful texts and calls in return. Diligent and consistent in her efforts, yet purposefully unobtrusive, Rachel had found a way to show she really cared. The fact that Ana started to care in return was icing on the cake. To have them moving to Collinsville was great news.

"Your buddy, Gilbert, is moving to Collinsville," Rachel said grabbing Skylark to do a little dance. "And, to think, just a few months ago when we first heard Jaime and his family needed a little help, my first reaction was 'I don't want to help anyone else.' Think of all the joy that would've been missed had I listened to that voice!"

"That was your first thought?" Cody asked, surprised. "I never would've known it from your response."

"It's embarrassing, but yeah. After everything with Susan and living in the city, I was tired and ready to just go home. I know it's human to feel the need to go inward and protect yourself, but this shouldn't have been one of those times. It's the tender direction of Holy Spirit that helped me quickly see my error in judgment and soften my heart. I'm so grateful for that."

"Hallelujah," Cody said in agreement. Then with a goofy grin, he added, "I had the same initial reaction."

The day after they returned home to Collinsville, Cody received a call from Dan. Initially it was to go over the projects for the next week. An opportunity for Cody to present how his remote position was going to work. But, after some initial chit-chat, Dan made Cody an offer.

"As you know, I've got a number of new projects on the horizon. I value your expertise and I appreciate you as a businessman — you've proven to be a really right-minded, talented guy. You'd be surprised how seldom I find people like you in my line of work."

Rachel had watched Cody's face as she listened to the call on speaker. It was obvious what he was thinking. Humbled and shocked, he was grateful for the recognition. But after all the challenges they had been through for the job in Manhattan, she could tell he was wishing he would have had more confidence in himself and his abilities in the beginning. He had allowed the unfamiliar situation to make him question himself; when the very things that made him different, were the things that made him even more qualified and valued.

"Anyhow," Dan had continued. "I was wondering if you'd be willing to form a partnership of sorts. I'd like to hire you as a consultant indefinitely. You'll serve as the lead carpenter project manager — exactly what you've done on the current project, but you'll work directly with me. There won't be anyone like Simone in the mix."

After a long discussion about the realistic needs of the position, and the realization that at points there would be multiple projects requiring attention and oversight; they agreed Cody should consider hiring a small staff of his own to meet the demands of the partnership.

Hanging up the phone, Cody turned to Rachel and said, "Let's figure out how to hire Jaime."

Just as Cody and Rachel had hoped, Jaime's degree in engineering and strong resume in Arts and Craft made him a solid candidate for a visa. After discussing the situation with a friend from church who used to work at the State Department, they were confident they were on to something.

Jaime accepted immediately. The initial plan was for him to stay in the city to help execute Cody's plans on site. Then, realizing Dan's next project and many after were in the Hudson River Valley, it made more sense for him to be based closer to Cody. It all took time to flesh-out. Cody had to make some changes to his own business classifications. And they had to gather proof of Jaime's experience in Arts and Craft-focused jobs. Since many of them in the US had been under the table, it was a challenge to prove his employment. However, once they had everything compiled, it was relatively easy to finalize.

It was the question of the Ramirez family's willingness to move Upstate that had Cody and Rachel eagerly standing-by.

Now, with everything in place, Jaime would be making his way back from El Salvador and Ana, Gilbert, and baby Paz could prepare to make their way to Collinsville. It was a wonderful turn of events.

Rachel handed Cody his phone back.

"Let him know how excited we are," she said. "I'm going to let Ana know about the house for sale on the outskirts of town. It's been on the market for months, but is just adorable. I bet they could get a really good deal. Think about Gilbert going from their one-bedroom apartment to a big house on an acre of land! He'd feel free as a bird."

***

The morning of the Ramirez's move, Rachel found herself lying awake at 5:30 a.m. Still dark outside, the weatherman forecasted a pristine fall day in the high 40's. Snow wasn't predicted for a couple more weeks. Which was fine with her, because beautiful red, orange, yellow, and golden brown leaves covered the earth throughout Collinsville, making a stunning ground cover that she didn't want to let go of just yet.

Susan was scheduled to arrive around 10 a.m., so Rachel and Cody could go help Jamie and the family move-in. It was just days before Thanksgiving and Rachel's heart was full. She hoped to get them all settled in well enough that they would be ready and relaxed for the holidays. With all of the help pouring in from the community, it seemed like a realistic goal.

On visits to get to know the town, Ana and the kids had attended Collinsville Community Church a couple times with Rachel. They readily accepted the warmth and reception of church members, quickly making friends and a place within the community. It couldn't help but make Rachel think about when Melinda and her family moved themselves and the adoption agency to Collinsville.

The situation had quickly revealed itself as a mistake. Even the illegal adoption practices aside, Collinsville was no fit for them and they were no fit for Collinsville. Their dismissive reaction to the church and neighbor's efforts had been such a disappointment for Rachel. She felt responsible for their arrival and the tarnish they brought with them. Ever the optimist, she believed things would work out, until it was obvious they wouldn't.

Even though she had been burned in the past, she never hesitated with the Ramirez family though. It was clear they were a caring, hardworking family filled with humility and a love for God. Church members had a welcome party planned for the Friday night following Thanksgiving. A harvest themed event, planned by the congregation's women's ministry, Rachel was anticipating an endless table of delicious baked goods; putting her couple of pies at Thanksgiving to shame.

Out her window, Rachel could see a tinge of light brightening the horizon. She was not going back to sleep. Contemplating how best to use her time, she knew what she needed to do. Gently lifting the covers, she went to the bathroom to get ready. After an exciting night of hayrides, local apple cider, dancing under the stars, and playing carnival games at the church's fall fundraiser, the rest of the family was tuckered out and fast asleep. On a sheet of journal paper, she wrote a quick note:

> *Good morning, Mr. Brooks.*
> *Went to the park for a prayer walk. I'll be home before the kids get up. I love you.*
> *xoxo*

Stepping into the crisp fall morning, Rachel found a hidden memory trying to make its way to the front of her mind. Taking a deep breath of the refreshing air and closing her eyes, she found herself stepping out of Collinsville Hospital's automatic front doors. The memory whisked her back to the first morning in town after Aunt Cali's stroke.

It was unexpected and unsettling. That morning, just three years before, Aunt Cali laid unresponsive in a hospital bed and Rachel was filled with despair and uncertainty. Feeling so lost and alone, with no one to turn to, she had gone to the park in hopes of finding hope.

Familiar with prayer walks from her teens, but terribly out of practice, Rachel had stepped into the park with a broken heart and contrite spirit. Years of living on her own terms, focusing on things of the world, had left her feeling empty and off track. With Aunt Cali's fate uncertain, Rachel questioned whether she had the right to reach out to Him after so long; but she had nowhere left to turn.

The dark recollection surprised Rachel and brought her focus back to reality as she approached the park. It made her sad to remember herself in such a lost state. Then she realized, from the first morning she stepped foot in the park those three years ago, she was blessed with the knowledge that she was never alone.

Like *Alice Through the Looking Glass*, Aunt Cali's stroke had thrust Rachel into a scary, lonely place; but through the restoring love of Holy Spirit it delivered her out the other side into a whole new world teaming with love, life, and joy.

As she made her way across Main Street, Rachel walked slowly past of all of the shuttered businesses reminiscing on that difficult, but inspiring time. Busy these days with the many beautiful blessings she had received since, it had been a long time since she let herself dwell on the devastating loss of her dear Auntie Cali. It felt healing to give the grief space in her heart again.

Entering the park, a soft breeze greeted her at the gate. In contrast to the crisp air of the cool morning, the breeze dancing at her shoulders was warm and comforting. Rachel smiled at the welcome as her hair tossed about her face. Like a playful hug from an old friend, it called her to her favorite place of intimacy.

Rachel had a strong testimony of prayer and its power, no matter where it took place; but for her, the park was a place for divine conversation and connection unlike any other. The park was special, a sacred place.

The sound of sand and earth crunching under her feet was grounding as she began to focus inward and prepare to pray. Approaching the lake she found herself looking for H.S., Holy Spirit. She always did. Even when she came to the park with the family or just the kids, she looked to see if He had returned for a visit — like He did that morning so long ago.

Ever since that day in the park three years ago, she hoped she might get the chance to spend more time with Him. She wanted to sit with Him, talk with Him, and have Him remind her *everything's going to be okay.*

After a good scan, she was pretty confident there was no one else around.

The lake was still and placid. She recalled seeing the high school's cross country team stretching for a practice run that morning in the park. No one was out today. No one was on the lake. It was too early for anyone to be pedal boating. Rachel figured so close to Thanksgiving people were busy.

Her heart reminded her that He was always with her. She knew it. It was just that it would be nice to have a conversation with Him again. Looking around, she appreciated having the space to herself. The intense quiet offered solitude perfectly suited for prayer.

A little sparrow suddenly jumped out of the shrubs along the trail, fluttering to a nearby tree, breaking the silence, and startling Rachel.

She jumped and began to giggle, laughing at herself. Reaching her favorite bench, she took a seat, and composed herself.

"Lord, thank you so much for the time this morning. These opportunities to talk don't come as often as I'd like and I'm so grateful to be here with You now," Rachel paused, considering what she really wanted to say. Opening her eyes, she stared out to the lake, her heart still wishing she would see H.S. pedal by. Shaking the thought out of her mind, she took a deep breath.

"Lord, thank you so much for blessing Susan with more time here on Earth. This morning, thinking back to when I lost Aunt Cali, I didn't think I was going to make it through. After losing my mom and losing so many years with my dad, to have her taken so early was a blow I didn't think I'd survive. I have a testimony that the loving comfort of Holy Spirit can help me through anything. I know anything's possible through you, Lord. But, I'm grateful that I get to keep her for now."

She took a deep breath, feeling overwhelmed with all that she had to be grateful for. Getting to her feet, she continued to talk to God, thanking him for everything that had happened with Cody's work, the move back to Collinsville, with the Ramirez family, and with Tom.

"I'm so grateful for the changes you've made in Tom's life," she said. "I look back on my life with him and it's was filled with so much *stuff*...money, work, material objects, superficial things with so little substance. I always felt the void and thank goodness I had the foundation to finally understand what was missing. Because of your loving guidance, I could see clearly and put you first moving forward. I'm glad Tom is getting that opportunity now."

She smiled. "I can only hope to be as patient and loving as you. As I learn to parent Sky and Slater, I hope to learn from all that you have done for me."

As the morning light filled the sky, Rachel spotted a teddy bear sitting along the path's curb. If she didn't know better, she would have sworn it was her Teddy from when she was 6 years old. Picking up the doll, she gently ran her fingers over his black stitched nose and glassy, marble-like eyes. She wondered whatever became of her Teddy. She imagined he just disintegrated from her constant attention; but she had no recollection of the last time she held him in her arms.

"Someone's going to miss you," she said, sitting him on a nearby bench.

She thought back to dancing with her Teddy on the fire escape of her family's Queens apartment. Driven out her window to avoid her parent's arguments, it was where she met Angel and in retrospect had her first spiritual experience. One of Heavenly Father's many tender mercies in her life, He was letting her know, even at that young age, she wasn't alone and that everything was going to be okay.

Patting the teddy bear on the head, she felt another rush of air encircle her. Turning into the warm breeze, Rachel put out her arms and closed her eyes. She twirled and swayed, dancing in the wind and reveling in His presence.

She opened her eyes and giggled as she spotted a pair of squirrels eyeing her from across the way.

"What?" she asked, laughing to herself.

As the sky grew brighter, she knew the kids would be getting up soon. Cody had gotten up with Slater in the middle of the night, after he had kept pace with Skylark at the Harvest Festival, so Rachel felt he deserved the morning off — before she put him to work moving heavy furniture. *Just a little bit longer*, her heart yearned.

Feeling like she hadn't had enough time to say all that she wanted to or listen for His response, she decided to stay just a bit longer.

Contemplating her childhood, it made her sad. It ended so abruptly at 14, when her mom died. Cali did everything right. But, basically orphaned, Rachel never felt like she was a normal teen.

She suddenly found herself in the grove where she and Cody made their wedding vows. Surrounded by shimmering fall leaves dancing in the breeze, it was a stunning space.

"Cody," she said with a smile. She thought back to when they met at Collinsville High School.

In all of her advanced classes, he appeared so confident, almost cocky. She despised how easily he seemed to get things right. It wasn't until she saw him at church with his grandparents, and helping another elderly gentleman to his seat, that she realized he was a good guy. Soon after they became friends, realizing the similarities in their situations — Cody being raised by his grandparents and Rachel, her aunt.

She fondly thought back to their unexpected reunion and whirlwind courtship, right after Aunt Cali's death and her breakup with Tom. She bowed her head with gratitude.

"Thank you, Lord," she said softly. "For blessing me with so much. I'm so grateful for my family. So grateful, that I think only you can understand my love for them. It's as though all of the heartache and all of the trials have lead me to a place where I understand nothing can be taken for granted. Having lost so many people that I love, I love these people everyday with everything I have. Having lived through a childhood with fear, insecurity, and abandonment, I understand how to make my children feel safe and loved. And, dear Heavenly Father, having lived without You in my life, I know what it means to say, 'I was blind, but now I see.'"

She rounded a corner on her favorite path and had a clear view of the lake. The soft blue sky reflected in its' still waters made it hard to tell where one ended and the other began.

"Okay, Lord," she sighed, heading back to her favorite bench for just a minute. "I'm sorry I've filled all of our time. I'm just really grateful for the place we're in right now. Help me to build-up those around me and share your love and light. Make me a great mom. Make me a great wife. Please use me to answer the needs of others. Let me be your messenger and give me the strength to accomplish your will. I'm listening. I love you. Amen."

Taking a seat, she closed her eyes and took in all of the sounds around her. The birds chirping softly, still chilly in the gentle morning light, the squirrels foraging in the fallen foliage, and the distant sound of others in the park jogging, talking, laughing.

"It's a beautiful day, isn't it?" a familiar voice acknowledged.

Rachel was awe struck.

"Oh, H.S.!" she exclaimed. "I've missed you."

"It's good to see you, too," He said. "You do know I've been with you all along, right?"

Overcome with emotions, Rachel began to cry. "Yes, I know," she hesitated. "It's just…"

"I know," He interjected. "It's hard to always *remember*."

"Yeah," Rachel sighed, wiping away a tear. "When things get really hectic and challenging, it's hard to feel You near or hear You."

"Darn nerves," He replied with a chuckle. "They do tend to act like earplugs."

Rachel smiled. His voice was healing, comforting. She felt loved.

"I was with you, here, when you and Cody got married. Do you remember?"

She nodded.

"I was with you every night that you two stayed up late discussing what to do about Skylark's adoption."

Rachel sighed. "Yeah, I don't know how we would've survived without You."

"I'm with you when you feel alone, scared, happy, overwhelmed, all of it," He said, pausing.

After a moment, He added. "I know this time can be overwhelming. Motherhood can be hard. The never-ending days, long nights, constant demands, can seem all encompassing. And, more often than not, the work goes unnoticed and unappreciated by those around you, especially the little ones you're giving everything to. Please remember, Motherhood is a divine partnership with God and I want you to know, you're doing a good job. You *are doing God's work.* I am with you always, helping you along, comforting you in times of need, and cheering you on when the days get long. I love you, Rachel. And, I know you love Me."

***

Rachel hoped Cody and the kids would be awake soon. After her beautiful experience, receiving exactly what she had hoped and prayed for, she had been reminded of just how blessed she truly was. She couldn't wait to see her family.

After spending time contemplating her own childhood trials and sorrow, Rachel felt she had made progress working through a lot of the pent-up heartache and sadness. Years of questions and loneliness from her dad leaving when she was only 6, her mom dying when she was 14, and Cali dying when she was 27, had left her with an internal shell of fear and unresolved pain. After spending time with Holy Spirit, she had a full understanding of His plan for her and a testimony of His healing power. She had been making progress on her own, but she felt His inspiration facilitated a perception beyond her own ability. Enlightened and energized, she was ready to take hold of the kids and Cody and give then all a big hug…they'd be lucky if she ever let go.

Smiling at the thought, she quickly made her way back down the gravel driveway. Her rapid footsteps crunched and kicked the rocks causing quite a ruckus. She figured if they weren't already awake, they would be soon.

Filled with love, strength, and peace, Rachel's soul was filled with His light, plus all of the divine support and love she could ever ask for. She felt whole, having a perfect understanding of her purpose, and the knowledge that she was a beloved daughter of God. She was eager to do His work and love her family.

Her heart beat rapidly as she approached the front door. Grasping the handle lightly, she pushed it open.

Immediately greeted with the happy babble of Cody and kids in the kitchen, funky Western music playing on the stereo, and the scent of pancakes and bacon, Rachel's heart leapt with joy.

Rounding the corner, she found Cody dancing with Slater in a carrier on his chest and Skylark twirling at his feet. Expertly flipping pancakes and sipping coffee while he happily entertained the kids, he was a sight that could melt even the coldest heart.

"Mama!" Skylark shouted excitedly, spotting her in the hall.

"Hey, Mama!" Cody repeated playfully. "Come over here and give Dada a smooch."

"Mama, Mama!" Skylark continued.

Rachel raced toward them, sweeping Sky into her arms and leaning in to give Cody a big kiss.

"I missed you guys," she said, kissing the top of Slater's head. "I'm so glad to be home."

Slater started to coo and hum as they all stood together. "Mmm-am, ah," he blew from pursed lips. "Mmmm. Mm."

Cody's eyes grew three sizes. "Did he just say mama?"

"I'll take it!" Rachel said, laughing.

Skylark put her little hands on Rachel's cheeks, directing her face to look her in the eyes.

Rachel giggled. "Yes, my dear?"

"Mama," Sky repeated lovingly, patting Rachel's cheeks.

Rachel laughed, feeling tears come to her eyes. "Yes, my love. *Mama,*" she replied softly. The weight of the word filled her heart and she was humbled to have such a sweet responsibility.

Cody handed her a cup of coffee and grabbed her by the waist. As they all danced together, she could feel Holy Spirit in the midst of their warmth.

The music slowed and Cody pulled her and Sky in for a group slow dance.

"How was the park?" he asked softly.

Rachel smiled and tilted her head, at a loss for words.

He returned the smile, knowingly. Brushing a stray hair from her face, he said, "I know. I can see His light in your eyes."

"At times we all feel lost…but then He reminds us we are never alone."

— Tammy Hotsenpiller

## OVERCOME TEMPTATION & SETBACKS
# WHEN YOU FEEL LOST

Here are five things I do when I am personally tempted or struggling in any way.

**Step One: Armor Up!**

Did you ever stop to ask yourself what's up with the armor illustration in the bible? I mean really unless you are trying to make a new fashion statement, or starting a new fitness trend, it's a bit over the top. Or is it? I for one could actually use some armor from time to time. Let me explain what I mean.

There have been times when I am in the middle of a temptation or personal crisis that I stop dead in my tracks and visually put this armor on piece by piece. It goes something like this.

Jesus, I need you really badly right now. So I will put on the belt of truth and not listen to the lies I am hearing. I will strap on my salvation helmet, because I know I am safe and secure in You. Help me to think the thoughts You have for me.

I put on the breastplate of righteousness to cover my heart and I ask You to guard my emotions.

I put on the sneakers of peace so that I walk in Your way alone.

I will use Your Word as my sword and ask that You fill me with Your Holy Spirit.

And last but not least, Oh God, I pick up the shield of faith, for I know no weapon formed against me can prosper.

So you see by the time you have equipped yourself with the armor of God you are covered from head to toe with God's protection.

If you are in the middle of temptation, or a personal

trial…then Armor Up friend.

> **The Armor of God:** "Finally, be strong in the Lord and in his mighty power. [11] Put on the full armor of God, so that you can take your stand against the devil's schemes. For our struggle is not against flesh and blood, but against the rulers, against the authorities, against the powers of this dark world and against the spiritual forces of evil in the heavenly realms. Therefore put on the full armor of God, so that when the day of evil comes, you may be able to stand your ground, and after you have done everything, to stand. Stand firm then, with the belt of truth buckled around your waist, with the breastplate of righteousness in place, and with your feet fitted with the readiness that comes from the gospel of peace. In addition to all this, take up the shield of faith, with which you can extinguish all the flaming arrows of the evil one. Take the helmet of salvation and the sword of the Spirit, which is the word of God." — *Ephesians 6:10-17*

## Step Two: Create an Accountability Team

In the multitude of counselors there is wisdom (Proverbs 11:14)…and that does not mean me, myself and I. God knows we all need some wisdom from time to time. Especially when we are emotionally tempted or spiritually hurt. I have a group of girlfriends that are my 'go-to gals'. They know me so well, maybe even better than I know myself at time. The key to this group of friends is to allow them permission to be honest with you even when you have convinced yourself "you're fine". Sometimes by simply talking through the issues you can avoid a serious mistake or decision.

**Step Three: Discern the difference between 'What's Good' and 'What's God'**

As a Life Coach and ministry leader I have had my share of meetings with people. I have to laugh how often someone tries to convince me God is telling him or her to "do this" or "do that." "Seriously Tammy, this is just too good to not be of God."

In all fairness I have done the same thing.

But come on now, there are times that the opportunity is just so good that it must be from God, right? Wrong! We can talk ourselves into anything we really want. So here is my advice. Ask yourself, "Why you think it's from God?" Now, break down every part of the decision into 'what if' questions. Be honest with yourself and then be patient enough for God to show you if it is from Him or from you. The truth is, not every open door is from God.

**Step Four: Choose Wisely**

So often we pray for guidance and discernment from God and then turn around and look for the answer we want to hear. We ask the question: Should I take the job, marry the guy, step into the responsibility, relocate cities, hang with the group... *yada yada yada* only to do what we wanted in the first place. Often temptation and personal trials are a direct response to our choices.

**Step Five: Prayer Walk**

This one gets me every time. Maybe because I have built up such an honest relationship with Holy Spirit on my prayer walks throughout the years, but I truly hear from God when I pray in the park. Now, I just might be a little bias to this form of praying but truly whatever works for you...just do it.

God has a way of speaking to our hearts when we seek His direction.

A few suggestions for a prayer time are:
- On your drive to and from work.
- Before getting out of bed in the morning.
- Your bathroom (this was my only place of solace when my children were small).
- When you are in the shower.
- Before you go to sleep at night.
- When you workout.
- On your lunch break.

# REFLECTIVE
# QUESTIONS

Ten Questions to ask yourself when you feel lost and overwhelmed.

**1. Have I come through tough times before?**

The answer for all of us is YES! It may seem like you will never get through this trial, but I promise you friend this, too, will pass. Reminding yourself that you have indeed come through difficult times will empower you to keep going.

**2. Can I see anything good coming out of this difficulty?**

My husband likes to call setbacks and poor decisions 'paying my tuition'. If I learn something or someone grows through my struggle then good came from it. Often the best lessons learned are because of hard times.

**3. Who can I talk to right now that will give me perspective?**

Don't sit and sulk in your sorrow. Get up and find someone to speak life into circumstance. A new perspective is often all we need to get through the phase we are in.

**4. What are three things I have right now to be thankful for?**

Keep a thanksgiving list. Why is it that we only celebrate Thanksgiving in November? We should have an attitude of gratitude…year round. It is amazing when we count our blessings we seem grow in joy.

### 5. Am I getting the proper rest and nourishment during this situation?

This one is so important. I remember when the phrase 'Hangry' came out. I thought brilliant. Yes! Someone gets it. I am hungry and that makes me angry. Friend…get smart take care of yourself. If you don't, no one else will.

### 6. Have I asked Holy Spirit to guide and comfort me?

I'm sure this should be #1 on our list but for some reason most of us think of Holy Spirit after we have tried all other means…So please feel free to ask yourself this question first. Holy Spirit is called our comforter in the Bible. He is our ever-present help in times of trouble. Ask H.S. to come and comfort and lead you into peace and truth.

### 7. Have I surrounded myself with positive healthy resources?

Here are a few examples:
• Worship music
• Positive Podcasts
• Church
• Good Friends

### 8. Will worry, anger, or regret really help at this time?

Of course the answer in NO! But for some reason we by nature turn inward and lick our own wounds. This will never, (I repeat…NEVER help). Step out of this dark place and see yourself taking healthy steps into your future.

### 9. Am I controlling my thoughts and actions?

You are better than this friend. I know you are. If we don't take our thoughts captive, they will be controlling our actions. I have several scriptures and quotes that I have memorized that are my 'go to place' when I feel overwhelmed. They help carry me out of the dark place of my soul. The key is meditating long enough on these truths to get you back on solid ground.

**10. Am I rested? Am I getting the rest I need?**
This one is an automatic NO for most people…lol. But in all seriousness it is so important. When we feel lost and overwhelmed most of us run. We run from the truth, we run from our friends, we run from ourselves. Let me encourage you to do something else. REST! Take the time you need to just simply be. Just press into the love and nature of a very good God and let Him bring rest, repair, and renewal. This will pass my friend, and the sooner you let go of what you think should happen and just rely on God's plan for the situation…the quicker you will feel normal again.

28587402R00140

Made in the USA
Lexington, KY
19 January 2019